No Less Worthy

A Young Adult Novel

By

DORCHELLE T. SPENCE

www.urbanedgepublishing.com

DEDICATION

For girls and women everywhere: although our challenges differ, we all struggle. In your struggle, remember that you are stronger, smarter, and braver than you think. Believe fiercely in your value as a person and in your ability to reach your destination no matter how difficult the journey.

ACKNOWLEDGMENTS

First, I give honor to God for giving me this story to tell. Writing this book has been a journey of growth and I appreciate my family and friends for supporting me along the way. Most especially, I thank Robert, my husband and best friend, for his patience, love and acceptance throughout this process and always. His unyieldingly honest assessments of my writing, even when it was difficult, made this an even better novel. I am grateful to the principals of UrbanEdge Publishing for believing in this story; to my editors, Rose Walker and Shae Anderson, for the clarity and laser-focus they brought to the project; and to my early critics, Emmanuel and Maggie, for their insight and candid feedback. It is because of each of you that I was able to maneuver through this phase of my life's journey. I am forever in your debt.

CHAPTER ONE

My arm throbbed from the strength of his grip. As he half-dragged me through endless rows of filthy tractor trailers, it became increasingly difficult to keep up. Voices surrounded us, their origin unclear. I could hear people shouting, flesh hitting flesh, metal slamming against metal, clawing fingernails, pleading cries, and unbridled groans that made my skin crawl.

My head jerked around searching for the source of each sound as they spun past and circled back for another assault. People were everywhere, there were bare legs intertwined or kneeling, groping hands in open shirts or beneath skirts too short for their wearers, pedestrians staggering or leaning – yet, I was alone with this stranger and the deeper he pulled me into the gulf of parked trailers, the faster my heart raced. The discarded wrappers with contents oozing from within, slimy oil spills, and nasty abandoned clothes combined with the stench of urine and other bodily fluids to make my stomach lurch.

Although I really didn't want to find out, I couldn't help wondering where the man was taking me and, all these years later, I still wondered how I had gotten myself into this.

* * *

"Wake up, Kathy! It's Christmas!"

1

Margaret Ann was jumping up and down at the foot of my bed.

Without opening my eyes, I swung at her legs. "Get off my bed!" I said through clinched teeth.

"Come on, Kathy, wake up," she continued happily, undeterred.

"I'm asleep. Leave me alone." I swung again.

"But we can open our presents now!"

I grunted and pulled the covers over my head.

"Kathy, pleeease."

"Oh, alright," I relented, throwing back the covers, causing her to fall. While she flailed giggling, I stretched and rolled out of bed. Grabbing my robe, I raced past her and into the living room.

Our apartment had been decorated since Thanksgiving and the presents were under the lopsided synthetic tree. As of last night, my sister and I each had three boxes.

"Ya'll up already?" Mama yawned in our direction rubbing her eyes with the back of one hand, holding a warm Coke can in the other. She hadn't bothered to put on a robe and her elongated breasts hung loosely beneath the thin worn gown.

Margaret Ann jumped up and ran to Mama who hugged her tightly. "Where's Daddy?" Margaret Ann asked when Mama released her.

"He'll be by later," she said tousling Margaret Ann's long kinky curls.

I rolled my eyes. Johnny Ray was never around for the big stuff. "Go on, open your presents," Mama said shooing Margaret Ann away with her free hand. The two of them were a little too excited for me at this ungodly hour of the morning.

Perched on the arm of the stained velour couch, Mama leaned across the coffee table reaching for her cigarettes. Tapping the package lightly against her

2

forefinger, she pulled one out and lit it. We watched her take a long satisfying drag. Blowing smoke, she nodded toward the overly tinseled tree lisping to the right.

Taking that as our cue, we rummaged through the gifts, passing boxes between us until we each had the three with our own names on it. In a flash, colorful wrapping paper flew here, there and everywhere.

I snatched opened the first box and squealed as a pair of blue jeans and a pink angora sweater fell out. "Oooh, Mama! Thank you!" My old jeans were hopelessly out of style. The frayed bottom was up to my ankle and the waist was snug, giving me an undeserved muffin top and making me look bigger than I am. I grimaced at the thought. It was hard enough flying under the radar of the mean girls at school without the outdated clothes. "Thank you, Lord," I whispered into the dark denim. I rubbed the soft fabric of the sweater across my cheek imagining my first day back at school after the break.

"It's Baby Alive!" Margaret Ann shouted. "I got a Baby Alive!"

Jarred by Margaret Ann's outburst, I tossed the box aside to see what else I'd gotten. I found my own blonde version of the same doll. Shaking my head, I pushed the box away. I eyed the last present with a combination of dread and hope. Taking my time peeling back the tape, I wondered if the box would reveal something else I could wear to school or another useless toy that I was too old for and had no interest in. I closed my eyes. Please let it be a skirt or dress, I prayed silently. Taking the lid off, I inhaled deeply and bravely peeked inside. Purple pajamas. Before exhaling, I glanced up to see if Mama was looking.

She was focused on Margaret Ann who'd gotten jeans, a purple sweater and a set of pink pajamas. It was exactly the same thing, right down to the baby doll. Whoo hoo, I thought wearily, another *great* Christmas.

Margaret Ann was bouncing from the doll to her pajamas to her jeans. Then she broke out into song – "Jingle Bells" – loud and off key. Mama used her cigarette as a conductor's wand to direct the chorus of one and I let my head drop. When she could no longer contain herself, she jumped up, pulling me with her, and together we went over to hug Mama.

"Thank you, Mama," we said in unison each kissing a cheek. Mama put her arms around the two of us, holding the hand with the cigarette away, so I could barely feel her. I wanted a real hug and leaned in closer.

But instead of hugging me to her, Mama pushed me away. "You're gonna make me burn you." I'd forgotten about the cigarette.

Still, my face flushed and I felt the sting of embarrassment as tears formed behind my eyelids. Hating for my emotions to show, I took a deep breath to steady myself. That's when I remembered. "Ooh, I almost forgot," I said running back to the tree. "This is for you." I returned with a small box wrapped in gold foil with green holly.

"For me?" Mama asked, feigning surprise.

"Yeah, it's from me and Margaret Ann." I winked at my little sister.

Margaret Ann bounced up and down clapping her hands as Mama slipped the cigarette between her lips and ripped open the package. The paper was off and across the room in one sweeping movement.

"Perfume!" Mama purred, causing her cigarette to wiggle and ashes to fall to the floor. She sprayed some on her wrist and we leaned in to smell.

"Umm, that smells good," we said together then laughed at the timing.

Mama took a drag, removed the cigarette, blew smoke from her nose, and then sniffed herself. "Oh, yeah, I like the smell of that. Thank you, girls."

It finally felt like Christmas to me, and we smiled at each other.

CHAPTER TWO

"And I have one more little thing for you, Margaret Ann," Mama beamed.

"For me?" Margaret Ann asked, giggling and bouncing again.

The anger rose so fast, I couldn't stop myself. "Why'd she get one more thing?"

Mama glared at me, her emotion matching my own. "Because she's the baby!" She quickly softened remembering that it was Christmas, "It's just a little something, Kathy My goodness."

She pushed herself up, speared the butt of the cigarette into the empty Coke can, and walked over to the TV stand. Our eyes followed. She returned with a small box wrapped in Santa Claus paper and handed it to Margaret Ann.

I hugged my doll to me and whispered into her ear, "I don't know why she gets 'one more little thing'," mimicking Mama.

"What did you say?" Mama glared at me.

"Nothing," I mumbled back.

Margaret Ann scraped at the paper trying to find a seam, but her young fingers were having a hard time and it was taking forever.

"Here," I said grabbing the box, "let me help you."

"No, I can do it! Give it back!" Margaret Ann reached for the box and I turned my body so that she couldn't reach it. "Give me! Mama!"

"I'm just trying to help."

"Kathy, give her the damn box!"

Startled, I threw the package into Margaret Ann's lap and flopped onto the couch with a loud huff. "I was just trying to help."

"Well don't," Mama answered as Margaret Ann finally pulled a piece of wrapping away.

"Oooh, you got a Nintendo DS," I said, impressed that Mama even knew about them. "Can I see?"

"No! It's my DS!"

I stood up to get a better look. The screen lit up and the animated voice invited her to play. Margaret Ann tried to push the buttons to make the girl on the screen move, but the screen went black instead. Margaret Ann didn't understand that the game needed to be charged and her frustration with it offered me a modicum of satisfaction. I chuckled as she pressed random buttons, shook the device, flipped it around and around and eventually tossed it aside. I was surprised that she didn't stomp it into the ground. I thought I showed great restraint in not laughing out loud.

"I don't even like this DS," she said walking past the spot where it lay on the thin gray carpet. "I'm gonna play with my Baby Alive."

"Can I see it then?"

"No Kathy," Mama answered quickly. "Just leave it alone. She'll play with it later."

"Well, if she's going to play with it later, maybe she should charge it," I replied smartly.

7

"Alright, miss smart ass. *You* go charge it. And you'd better not do anything else with it either."

With a sigh, I picked up the electronic handheld game, removed the adapter from the box and plugged it into the wall.

Margaret Ann watched this interaction from the Christmas tree; when the smoke cleared and I'd plopped back onto the couch, she shyly sauntered over. "Kathy," she sang innocently, "Wanna play mommies and babies?" I was familiar with the voice. It was her way of apologizing for getting me into trouble.

My aggravation had lessened, and I had to admit that I was a bit bored. Aware that it was Christmas, I gave in to the moment. There was no point in making her suffer for Mama's unfair treatment of me. I should be used to it by now anyway. Walking over to the tree, I stooped over to get my doll and began to remove it from the box.

"Uh," Mama said, as if struggling to understand what she was seeing. "And just what do you think you're doing?"

I looked up, confused. Surely she just heard Margaret Ann ask me to play. "Getting ready to play dolls with Margaret Ann."

"She can go play," Mama answered waving a hand toward Margaret Ann. "But you need to clean up this living room and get dinner started. It'll take hours for that turkey to bake."

I sucked in a breath to keep the deep throaty growl I felt coming up through my soul from spewing forth and getting me further into Mama's danger zone. But I feared it was already too late. She was in rare form today, probably since Johnny Ray hadn't shown up.

"You're about grown now, Kathy," she continued. "You need to start pulling your weight around here. I'm sick and tired of taking care of your ungrateful ass." Johnny Ray had better get here soon.

8

CHAPTER THREE

"Yes ma'am," I mumbled, putting down the doll and making my way into the adjacent kitchen to get a trash bag. Stuffing the discarded wrapping paper and ripped cardboard boxes into the bag reignited my smoldering anger. Why would she buy a fourteen-year-old a doll anyway? And pajamas. Really? Who sleeps in pajamas? Hadn't she even noticed I was a teenager? She could have spent that money on another pair of jeans or a shirt or something I could have really used. I only got new clothes twice a year as it was – on Christmas and my birthday. Everything else was handed down from a cousin or one of her friend's children or bought from the thrift store. Was I that invisible? Couldn't she have stopped thinking about Margaret Ann for five minutes and given a little bit of thought to her first born? Humph. The truth was, Mama had stopped thinking about me a long time ago. And that was what hurt so badly.

In the kitchen, I dumped the trash bag, washed my hands and took out the 10 bunches of turnip greens I'd picked and cleaned the night before while Mama and Margaret Ann sang Christmas carols and ate the popcorn I was going to string for the tree. For a while, I stood watching the boiling chicken broth mixture, feeling its heat on my face, allowing the steam to cloud my vision and sting my eyes. It concealed the tears, if anyone cared to look. No one did. Finally, I turned away from the turnip greens and focused on preparing the turkey for baking and peeling the sweet potatoes for the candied yams.

With dinner cooking, I avoided the living room where Mama sat talking on the phone and slipped past the bedroom where Margaret Ann was playing. Instead, I made my way to the bathroom. Inside the small, cool, white-tiled space I twisted the door knob to muffle the sound of the door closing. Not bothering to turn on the light, I gripped the sides of the sink and let out the growl I'd been holding in. Turning my head to the left, I caught a whiff of my underarm. Eww. I was badly in need of a shower.

I stripped down, leaving my clothes where I'd been standing and started the shower. While the water heated, I brushed my teeth and gargled. I spit, then caught a glimpse of myself in the mirror. My light brown eyes held a glint of gold that matched the scattering of freckles around my high cheeks and thin round nose. My brown hair was so dark it looked black and a couple of days without shampoo had turned my soft, wavy curls into long, straight strands of silk that framed my pale, oval shaped face. I looked more white than black, but more exotic than the typical white girl.

On days when I could be kind to myself, I knew that I was pretty, maybe even beautiful in some ways. Strangers on the street stopped to tell me that. Their generous compliments made me feel self-conscious and guilty, especially when Margaret Ann was around. They hardly noticed her presence and never complimented her. I always made an effort to acknowledge her, but I couldn't tell if she cared or not. Margaret Ann's look was so different from mine that I often had to convince people that we were sisters.

Her milk chocolate skin appeared darker next to my creamy complexion. Her eyes were the size and color of chocolate tootsie pops and the mess of unruly brown hair that felt more like wool than cotton gave her a monochromatic look. It didn't help that Mama never bothered to comb her hair, and my efforts to tame the mane were met with blood curdling screams. But Margaret Ann's smile was infectious. It lit up her entire face and brought happiness to everyone who took the time to see it.

I wondered who I made happy. Apparently no one. I climbed into the shower. Why did everything fall on me to do? When did I become the grown up? And if I was the grown up, then why didn't I have any of the freedom that was supposed to come with being an adult? I stood with my head beneath the shower spout letting the water run down my face and drown out my thoughts. I soaped and rinsed twice before washing my hair.

Toweling off and feeling fresher, I decided to give the day a new start. I wrapped myself in the towel, slipped out of the bathroom and into the bedroom I shared with Margaret Ann to get dressed.

She smiled as I entered the room. "Play with me now?" she asked.

"Sure. Let me put the turkey in the oven, then we'll hang out."

For a while, I found myself caught up in the magic of the day. We played mommies and babies and Uno and built a castle out of sheets and chairs and pillows. We pretended to be princesses and held a royal ball where we danced around the room to whatever songs played on the radio. Margaret Ann had much better rhythm than me and tried to teach me the latest line dances. It was a fiasco, and she was often rolling on the bed with laughter. I definitely had two left feet. I was so bad; I had to laugh at myself.

"Kathy!" Mama called a little while later.

"Yeah?"

"Ain't this dinner ready, yet? I'm hungry."

I tickled Margaret Ann and left the room. Thirty minutes later the table was set, the rolls were out, and dinner was ready to be served.

"Ya'll come to the table," I called as the sun set and my energy waned.

Racing to the table, Margaret Ann tripped over the DS still on the floor next to the outlet.

"I hate this stupid thing," she whined, rubbing her foot.

"Can I have it then?" I asked, unplugging the console and picking it up.

"No, Kathy, you can't have her present," Mama answered, her temper flaring.

"But she doesn't want it. She doesn't even know how to work it."

"I do too know how to work it!"

I wanted to choke her for opening her mouth. This was between Mama and me, and she needed to stay out of it. Instead, I held the game out to her. "Then show me," I challenged.

"I don't have to show you anything."

"That's because you don't know how to work it."

"I do too!"

"You're such a whiner!"

"Am not!"

"Are too!"

Mama slammed her palm on the table. Startled, Margaret Ann and I both jumped.

"Both of y'all shut up! And for the last time, Kathy, no, you can't have it. So put that damn game down and make Margaret Ann's plate."

I slammed the game on the counter. And as if I had physically assaulted her, Mama lunged at me. It was all I could do to avoid her right hand.

"Mama!" Margaret Ann screamed.

"What!" Mama glared at me, chest heaving, breathing labored.

"This isn't fair," I shouted, regaining my speech. "You always treat her better than me! It's like you only love her. Like she's the only one who exists to you!"

"She's the baby! Why don't you understand that?"

"Oh, I do. I do understand that. And I understand that she gets whatever she wants and she does whatever she wants while I get stuck in here doing your cooking and cleaning while you talk on the phone complaining about everything you have to do around here. I understand a lot more than you think!"

"You don't understand nothing!" she said stepping closer to me. I nervously stood my ground.

"Yeah? Well, I understand that if my daddy was here, you wouldn't be treating me this way."

And wham! There it was. Mama slapped me – hard – across the face. I gasped, choking back burning tears. I wouldn't let myself cry. I refused to give her the satisfaction. But Margaret Ann couldn't help herself. She was openly crying as if it were she who had been hit.

"Mama!" she screamed again.

"No! That girl makes me sick!" Mama spat. "You ain't got no Daddy!" Mama struggled to catch her breath as the words tumbled forth. "Whoever he was, he was around just long enough to get what he wanted. As far as I'm concerned that man is dead and gone, and he ain't never coming back. You can sit your ass down and shut your smart mouth or you can go to your room for the rest of the night. I don't really care what you do!"

13

Still holding my face, I turned to leave, but my pant leg got caught on the chair. In my struggle to break free, the chair toppled and I could no longer hold back the tears. I was full-out sobbing by the time I slammed the bedroom door behind me. Throwing myself onto the bed, I buried my face into the pillow and screamed, "I hate this place".

The door snatched open and, terrified, I looked up to see Mama's face darkly stern, her eyes boring into me. "And when you wake up," her voice was low and painfully clear, "you gonna clean this kitchen and take out this garbage." The door closed with a thud and I let my head drop.

I laid there collecting myself and replaying the scenes from the day over and over. I'd gone too far, crossed the line. And so had she. She'd hit me in the face. She'd never hit me in the face before. There was nothing left for me here now. Nothing would ever be the same again.

My fingers reached between the mattress and box spring and fished out my journal. There was so much noise in my head trying to get out. I couldn't write fast enough. I fell asleep with the journal in my hand and a lot still on my mind.

CHAPTER FOUR

The next morning I rose before the sun. "I hate this place" rang loudly in my ears and I knew what I had to do. I eased back the covers and slid silently out of bed. Tiptoeing over to the dresser, I carefully pulled open a drawer and took out my new jeans and sweater, as well as a pair of old sweat pants and my overalls. From another drawer I retrieved a long-sleeve pullover and a collared shirt. I began to put the items on one layer at a time until I felt as big as a department store Santa.

Bending over to put on my shoes, I slid off the weak mattress and onto the floor. Margaret Ann rolled over. I held my breath until her eyes closed, then reached for my shoes again, pulling them on, this time making as little noise as possible. Fully dressed, I got to my knees and used the bed to push myself up. Gliding to the door, I turned the knob.

"Where're you going?"

Fear gripped me and I jerked around feeling intense heat on my cheeks. "Uh…um…" I stammered. "To take out the trash."

"This early?" Margaret Ann yawned and wiped her eyes with the back of her hands. "The sun isn't even up yet."

"Uh…I want to surprise Mama."

"Oh."

I slowly pulled the door open, looked nervously toward Mama's bedroom, then lightly stepped down the hall to the kitchen. The trash can was overflowing, so I pulled out the bag, put on a twist tie, and inserted a new one. Unlocking the back door, I glanced around the dark kitchen with dishes piled in the sink. I guessed she expected me to wash them today. Humph. I sighed, opened the door and walked out.

On the street, I heaved the trash bag into the dumpster and listened as it hit with a thud. It sounded like the condition of my life. Heavy and flat. The wind was high outside, and I shivered as I stuffed my hands into the pockets of my overalls. There weren't many cars on the road as I made my way down the main drive of our apartment complex, took a left onto one of busiest east-west thoroughfares of our city and walked the half mile distance to the expressway on ramp. I wasn't sure where I wanted to go, but it was going to be far away from here. The quickest way I knew to put distance between me and this wreck of a life was to hitch a ride on a rig that was going across the Hernando DeSoto Bridge. "Go west, young woman, go west," popped into my head and I nodded at the thought. "Manifest destiny," I whispered.

An 18-wheeler rolled by and, defiantly, I stuck out my thumb. Its air horn sounded as it whizzed by. I walked farther up the ramp to I-40 with my thumb out. The wind whipped my hair and I lowered my shoulders into my sweater. Trucks swished past me pushing more cold air my way. My eyes leaked water.

I counted cars and watched mile markers to pass the time and to keep from thinking about what might be happening at home. Car traffic was starting to pick up. I decided to look for a particular model – Chevys – and was so busy finding them that I didn't notice the rig slowing down behind me.

The unexpected sound of the air horn caused my heart to nearly jump out of my chest. It beat like an African drum and my palms were suddenly moist. My mind raced but took me nowhere as I stared blankly at the asphalt.

"You coming?" boomed a man's voice.

I looked up and saw a mess of brown hair and bushy eyebrows.

"You coming or not?" he repeated impatiently.

"Uh---" I looked around for a sign from God, but all I saw were cars speeding past. I was on my own.

"Well, if you ain't goin' nowhere, what you out here for?"

I shrugged my shoulders and thought about it. He was right; this was what I wanted, right? Yes. I was out here in the freezing cold waiting for someone to take me away from the craziness of my life. "I'm coming."

The door swung open with a rush of warm air revealing an equally hairy arm and hand. Hesitating just a second, I grabbed it, climbed clumsily into the cab, and watched as the door was snatched shut behind me. I pressed myself into the back of the seat as the man's hand retreated across my body. I exhaled and tried not to touch anything, sitting as close to the door as I could without falling into the expanse between the seat and the door. Country music played and static voices flowed in and out of the dash board. Did they call it a dash board in a rig? I could feel the driver studying the side of my face and I dared not look over. Instead I kept my eyes on the grimy floor.

After what seemed like an eternity, he moved a gear and the truck hissed and bounced onto the expressway. When I thought the man was finally watching the road, I stole a glance in his direction. On the floor between us was a half-eaten box of chicken, a stack of CDs, and some papers on a clipboard, in the cup holder sat an Exxon coffee cup. The driver's dark blue jeans were stained and dirty as were his well-worn work boots. He wore a red vest over a predominately blue plaid shirt with the sleeves rolled up. His hands were huge and calloused and his thumbs stuck out oddly to the sides.

"So, where you goin' little girl?"

I jumped. His gruff voice startled me out of my thoughts.

"What you jumping for? You scared?"

"No, I'm not scared," I answered smartly. "You just startled me, that's all."

"So you're tough then, are you?"

"Yeah, I'm tough," I said, but even to my own ears I sounded small and scared.

CHAPTER FIVE

The driver looked at me and I scooted closer to the door. My senses were all on high alert and the inner voice I sometimes heard was screaming at me. Everything inside was telling me that I had made a big mistake getting into this truck.

"I ain't going that far," he said. "Today's my short haul only as far as Little Rock. Will that get you close to where you need to be?"

"Uh...yes," I said. "Little Rock is perfect." Little Rock was farther than I'd ever been from home. Only twice had I been across the 'M' Bridge with its graceful iron trestles that form the letter M which happens to be the first letter in Memphis, the city that sits on the east side of mile-long bridge and was – until now – my home. The two times I left the city only happened because Mama didn't have anybody to keep me while she, Margaret Ann, and Johnny Ray drove over to West Memphis to pick up a scrap car. Johnny Ray worked in construction, but to make extra money he would buy and sell scrap cars or car parts. I didn't know where he kept his scraps, but it wasn't in our apartment complex. It must have been with his other family.

"Uh huh," the driver said, bringing me back to the present. As he drove along, he took out a cigarette and lit it. It was the same brand Mama smoked, Filter King Kool. The scent reminded me of home.

Mama would know I was gone by now. Margaret Ann probably told her I'd taken out the trash. I wondered if she thought I'd been kidnapped. Probably not. Who would want to take me? Not even she wanted me around.

She has probably called the police, I thought. I wondered if the cops had their lights flashing when they came to the apartment. I bet they asked her what she did to make me runaway. They probably knew it was her fault. I bet she was sorry now.

"You hungry?"

I jumped again. I needed to stop letting my mind run free and focus on what was going on around me. I shook my head no, but my stomach argued with me and growled loudly to make its point. That was when I remembered that I hadn't eaten dinner the night before. If the driver hadn't mentioned it, I would've been fine. Why couldn't he just drive and leave me alone?

With his head, the driver motioned to the chicken box between us.

I kept my hands folded in my lap and ignored the food.

He grinned broadly, showing brown gums and uneven teeth, some missing altogether. I felt uneasy. I really needed to find a way out of his truck. "How far is Little Rock anyway?" I asked, studying the dirt on the floor board.

"About a hundred and fifty miles."

My head jerked up as I sucked in a wisp of air.

"Aw, it ain't that far. Just about three hours from where we are now."

I nodded. One hundred and fifty miles. Wow. I was going far away. But far was what I wanted, I remembered. The farther, the better.

We rode in silence across the Hernando DeSoto Bridge. I looked out the window and down at the Mississippi River below. The currents were moving fast. There were waves in it and white foam. It looked deep and angry, like me. I imagined it must be what the ocean looks like. Being suspended above the fast moving water frightened me and added to my growing anxiety about being in the rig at all.

A few miles into Arkansas, with the bridge a close memory and the dread growing deeper in the pit of my stomach cutting its own imposing channel, the driver pulled the rig off the road and into a truck stop.

"Why are we stopping?" I asked, my heart suddenly pounding loudly.

"I thought you was tough. Don't go gettin' all scary now." He pushed open the door and hopped down. On the ground his head was well above the seat of the rig when he looked back and grinned at me. That's one big man, I thought, feeling more uneasy by the second. When his door slammed shut, I contemplated my escape.

As he walked around the truck, I looked behind the seat for something I could use to defend myself, but my door was snatched open too soon. The driver grabbed my arm firmly and pulled me out of the cab. I screamed and squeezed my eyes shut as tightly as I could. "It's a little late for that, don't you think?"

I shook my head quickly from side to side. Please don't hurt me…Please don't hurt me…my mind chanted over and over, but my mouth didn't move. Fear had gripped every inch of me and rendered me mute. It was all I could do to walk and breathe. I made not another sound.

Someone behind us whistled. "Hey, Shortie. Ain't you a pretty young thing? Um hmm. I wish Santa had put something like you under *my* tree."

I turned my head in the direction of the voice, but the driver tightened his grip on my arm and I looked up at him instead. We were walking fast and he was half dragging me, so I couldn't catch up enough to see the expression on his face.

Behind us someone said, "Lips like yours would make a lollipop happy. Come on over to my truck; I've got a banana popsicle for you." It was a different voice that time, deeper and raspier. Hearing it made me feel dirty.

I inched closer to the driver, then realized that probably wasn't a smart move.

In front of us other men and women walked close together through the sea of trucks laughing and touching. They were mostly oblivious to us. Some of the women had on very short skirts with tall boots and tank tops. Others were in halter tops and shorts with high-heel sandals. They must be cold, I thought. One of them walked up to the man holding my arm. Was she coming to save me? I reached out to her with my eyes. Pleading: Help me; I'm in great danger. But she ignored me altogether.

"Hey, Big Daddy," she said zeroing in on the driver. "I can do you better than she can." The woman cut me a nasty look. I no longer wanted her to see my eyes. She wasn't coming to save me. No one was coming to help me. She adjusted to our pace, "I got what you need baby," she said stepping in front of the driver.

We brushed past her.

"Come on Big Daddy," the girl called after us. "Don't leave me like that,"

My heart was on the verge of exploding from the pressure fear was exerting on it. In desperation I forced my throat to open and my mouth to move. "Where are we going?" I pushed out breathlessly, trying again to see his expression, to discern his intent. The driver said nothing. Instead, he tightened his grip and dragged me forward. My arm was going numb and my bladder was full. I was going to wet myself.

We turned the corner on a row of rigs and saw a man with his pants down and a person stooping in front of him. It looked like the back of a man's head, but the person was clearly wearing a red halter top and green pleated skirt. I tried to see what was going on, but the driver pulled me back around the corner and we took a different direction.

Around the next corner a girl was crying from the shock of having been slapped hard across the cheek. I covered my face with my free hand. "You slut!" he shouted. "You ain't worth ten dollars; you're barely worth one."

As he stormed off, the girl shouted after him through sobs. "You sawed-off... pistol head... biscuit eating... son of a junk yard dog!"

Hot tears spilled down my own cheeks. My ears were tuned in to every sound of heavy breathing, the clanking of belt buckles and high- heels clacking, cat calls, screams, and shouts of elation. I no longer had to go to the bathroom. I no longer wanted to go to Little Rock. All I wanted to do was get as far away from this place and this man as possible.

The driver stepped up to the door of the truck stop. "Stay here," he commanded. "Don't move from this spot. And don't talk to anyone." He gave my arm an extra squeeze to make the point then released me and snatched open the door.

Instinctively, I looked down at my arm sure that a nasty bruise was spreading across my skin and that I would be able to see it through my sweater. The woman was beside me so fast that I felt her before I saw her. I felt her warm breath on my face. She was skinny and just a hair taller than me, which wasn't saying much considering she was wearing four inch stilettos.

I could smell the earth in her black leather jacket. She was a biker girl. This fact, along with her yellow face, long black hair, and the dragon tattoo on the side of her neck gave her an exotic look that I envied. She would be pretty, but for the crooked bottom teeth that made her lip protrude a little more than it should.

"What are you doing out here?" she asked urgently, standing too close for comfort. Her eyes bore into my soul.

Looking away, I fidgeted with my arm. "I don't know," I hedged, "escaping, I guess."

"This is not the way to do it. It's dangerous out here."

"You're okay," I answered defiantly.

"Looks can be deceiving. The people who look like they're on top of the world are sometimes the ones hurting the most."

I rolled my eyes. What did she know.

"Listen," she said grabbing me by the shoulders. I drew in a breath steeling myself against what would come. "I was just like you once," she continued. "Home sucked. My mom was a drunk. My dad beat her nearly half to death and then forced me to be his new wife. I thought anywhere would be better than there. I didn't know how wrong I was.

"I left home at 13. Met a guy and got in his truck. He even fed me. Humph. Only one little problem – the food was drugged. When I woke up, baby, men were all over me. I tried to get up – to run – but there was no way up. Nowhere to run. And that was just the beginning. It went on like that for months.

"Eventually, I was able to get away. But that dump just led to another dump. And now I'm stuck out here."

A woman staggered past us, disheveled and shaking. She was trying to catch up to a burly black man who was sauntering past us as if he were strolling down a red carpet somewhere in Hollywood. "Come on, man, just a hit," the woman called. "I just need a little bump." The man grinned and winked at me. I turned my head and the

24

woman in the leather jacket shifted us closer to the plate glass window of the truck stop.

"You don't want this life," she said, nodding toward the addict and her supplier. "Whatever is going on at home, believe me; it's ten times worse out here." She paused, sizing me up. "How old are you anyway?"

"Fourteen."

"Okay. You've only got four more years. I know that sounds like a lifetime right now. But it'll be over before you know it."

I looked down, studying a wad of gum that was grounded into the sidewalk.

"You can do it. Don't be like me. Be smarter than me. You have a future. Maybe you can even go to college."

I bit my lip. I did want to go to college. I did want to be somebody someday. I wanted to be like--- Her fingernails dug into my shoulder bringing me back to the present. "He's coming," she said roughly. "You've got to get out of here." As she walked off, her eyes locked with the truck driver.

He scowled at me. "I told you not to talk to anyone!" Snatching my arm, he drug me back through the lot.

"Why did you bring me here?" I shouted at him through tears.

"Because you needed to understand," he said roughly.

"Understand what?"

He yanked me around to face him. "You need to understand that these streets ain't no place for little girls. The people out here play for keeps and little girls either eat or get ate." He turned me around and marched me back past the rows of filthy rigs and evil deeds back to his truck. He snatched the door open with one massive hand and shoved me inside with the other. Wounded and finally free of his grip, I rubbed my sore arm again and tried to bring back the feeling while digesting what I'd seen and heard. Sounds rang in my ears in the stillness of the truck and I cried for each of the women I saw – and for me.

The driver paced angrily outside the front windshield of his rig, head down, muttering words I couldn't and didn't want to hear. I didn't know how many minutes had passed before the driver's door finally opened. I needed whatever minutes had been afforded me to get my own thoughts together and process the things I'd seen As he climbed back into the rig our eyes met and locked. After a few seconds, he shook his head breaking our silent communication and climbed in. "I'm taking you back to where I found you. What you do from there is up to you.

CHAPTER SIX

Sleet pelted the windshield of the rig and I could barely see the 'M' bridge as we crossed the Mississippi River back into Tennessee. A combination of precipitation and cigarette smoke fogged the windows and distorted the Downtown Memphis skyline giving it a foreboding look and intensifying my feeling of dread. Too soon the rig had come to a stop on the opposite side of the very same overpass a few miles from the Lake Crossing Apartments where Mama and Margaret Ann probably sat wondering where I was and when – if ever – I would return home.

The hairy driver stared straight ahead. I guessed he'd said all there was to say and it made little sense for me to linger. But as he drove away, I felt strangely alone and vulnerable. He was right, what I did from here was up to me. The question was: what was I going to do. The ice pellets started to stick. The wind and sleet stung my face. Despite shrinking further into my sweater, my eyes and nose were both running tears and mucus that instantly froze.

Not yet ready to go home, and wondering if I ever would be, I knew that the first thing I had to do was to find a place to ride out the storm. I remembered seeing a gas station a little ways back, so I walked in that direction. I saw the lights above the pumps long before I reached the convenience store. When I finally did, I could barely bend my fingers enough to pull open the heavy glass doors. My canvas shoes and thin socks had formed an icy partnership and together were solid blocks of ice. My mouth was clenched shut and I was grinding my teeth to keep them from chattering. Although I couldn't stop shivering, I was determined to get the door open.

Finally inside, the warmth of the store engulfed me like a welcoming hug and I began to cry. The clerk, who had been sitting behind the bulletproof glass reading a magazine, looked up.

"You alright?" she called through the mouthpiece.

My teeth chattered and my entire body shook. All I could manage was a nod.

"You don't look alright." The clerk stood and walked out of the room and into the store. "What's your name, baby?" Her voice was soft and calm.

"K-K-Kathy," I stammered.

She placed her arms around my shoulders. "You're freezing! What are you doing out in this weather? You'll catch your death of cold!"

The clerk stepped back to take a better look at me. The mucus in my nose had started to thaw and it oozed despite my best efforts to suck it in. I had managed to stop crying, but the physical and emotional toll of the day must have shown on my face.

She guided me gently into the small area behind the glass. "I'm not supposed to have anyone back here, but I've got an electric heater and you need it more than me. You sit right here," she indicated a stepstool near the heater, "and let it warm you up."

I wanted to hug her for being so nice, but my arms were wrapped around my own body and I was afraid to move them. Fresh tears spilled down my wind-burned cheeks.

28

"What's the matter, Miss Kathy?" She asked peering at me. "It can't be that bad baby."

I couldn't answer. I didn't trust my voice. And if I could answer, what would I say? As customers came and went, I sat still and quiet – sometimes crying, sometimes not – staring down at the heater before me, seeing and re-seeing things I wish I didn't. I had crossed a different kind of a line. I wasn't sure exactly when I crossed it though. Was it when I threw the trash bag into the dumpster and kept walking? Or was it when I got into the man's truck? I wasn't sure, but what I did know was that there was no easy way to go back.

"Are you feeling any better, Miss Kathy?" the clerk asked after a while.

I looked into her kind blue eyes, seeing her poorly cut, bleach blonde hair and thin dry lips. I smiled. "Yes ma'am."

She smiled back. "That's much better. When you first came in here, I wasn't so sure you were going to make it." She laughed, and it was a pleasant, friendly sound.

I almost asked if I could go home with her. But I knew better than that.

"Are you hungry, Miss Kathy? My shift's almost over, but I can get you something to eat before I get out of her."

Grateful for the offer I said, "Yes, please."

"Oh, you're so polite," she toussled my hair. I looked up at her and smiled for the first time in more than 24 hours. "What would you like? We've got some of those prepackaged chicken salad sandwiches in the back case, and you can even have a bag of chips and a drink if you want."

"Yes, thank you. I'd like that, please."

She winked at me, then left to get the things she'd mentioned. A male clerk entered the store and I saw her call him over. From behind the glass, I couldn't hear what they were saying. But because they kept glancing at the glass cage, I assumed she was telling him about me.

I smiled when the first clerk returned with the food. Although I was warmer, my fingers were still uncoordinated and I needed helping opening the packages. Even cold, that sandwich was very nearly the best thing I'd ever tasted and half of it was gone before I took a breath.

When I finally looked up, the clerk was watching me intently with a concerned look on her small, heart-shaped face. "Would you like to use the phone," she asked. "You could call someone to come get you."

I swallowed hard to force the rest of the sandwich down. I had been thinking about who I could call. Mama was out of the question. First, she didn't have a car, and second, I did not want to see Johnny Ray right now, or ever for that matter. The only person I could think of was Mama's sister, Grace, but that would make Mama even madder. Still, she was the only other family I had.

CHAPTER SEVEN

I dialed the number slowly using the extra seconds to figure out what I would say when she answered, if she was even still at that number.

"Hello?"

The chill started in my ear, gave me an odd sort of brain freeze, and followed my spine clear down to my ankles. I shuddered.

"Hello?" she repeated sharply.

"Um...Aunt Grace?" I held my breath hoping it was her and that she would remember me.

The line was silent. I closed my eyes and held on, willing her to know me. The last time I'd seen Aunt Grace I had been seven years old. We were at the hospital just after Margaret Ann was born. She had come to see the baby, but before Margaret Ann was brought in, Aunt Grace noticed Mama's black eye and swollen lip. She asked Mama what had happened. Unfortunately, Johnny Ray was standing there. Mama looked away and said she'd fallen. I sucked in my breath.

Aunt Grace didn't believe Mama and my reaction hadn't helped. Mama cut me an evil look and I studied the floor, remembering. The night before Margaret Ann was born, Johnny Ray hadn't come home. Mama was angry because she had been in pain and had needed to go to the hospital. But there had been no one to take her. She'd started calling everyone we knew, even Johnny Ray's friends, looking for him.

The next morning Johnny Ray had stormed into the house, opening the door with such force, the doorknob slammed into the wall leaving a hole. Mama had struggled to get to her feet, but before she could, he'd grabbed her by the arm and without a word dragged her into their bedroom. He'd slammed the door and Mama had let out an ear piercing scream. I'd thought he'd hit her and I'd run to the door and pounded on it, begging them to let me in.

There had been lots of shouting about Mama embarrassing Johnny Ray and loud crashes as furniture was overturned and glass was shattered. I could hear Mama crying and pleading with him to stop before he hurt the baby. He'd said he'd never wanted the baby in the first place and that she had used it to trap him. Even though they'd fought before, that was the first time his violent outbursts at Mama had reached that level and I'd been scared that he was going to kill her.

Suddenly, Johnny Ray had snatched open the door and I'd fallen into the room. He'd motioned as though he was going to kick me and I'd thrown my arms over head, covering my face, and held tight. But he turned instead and stomped out. I'd laid there a minute, too afraid to move, straining to hear footsteps or the door slamming or anything to tell me that Johnny Ray had gone.

In the quiet of the apartment, I'd started to panic. Where was Mama? Was she alright? Was the baby alright? I'd crawled over to where Mama lay and seen that she was bleeding from the nose and mouth. Her hands were wrapped around her stomach protectively, and she was still.

A wave of nausea had gripped me and I could barely hold down my cereal. I could taste the stomach acid and it had burned my throat. With every ounce of determination I could muster, I'd forced its contents back down and reached for Mama.

Aware of my presence, she'd whispered, "Kathy, call 911. The baby's coming."

My eyes had grown wide and my heart raced. The phone was all the way in the kitchen. I couldn't have just left Mama lying there like that. What was I supposed to do?

"Kathy," Mama had said sounding remarkably calm, "get the phone and dial 9-1-1. Tell the operator you need an ambulance. Your mama's having a baby."

I'd nodded, but still couldn't move my legs. In all the confusion, I couldn't remember if I'd heard the backdoor close or not. I couldn't remember hearing the sound of Johnny Ray's truck pulling off. Oh Jesus, I'd thought, what if he was still here? What if he wouldn't let me use the phone? What if he was still mad and had beaten me too? Worse, what if he had left but had come back to hurt Mama again?

As I'd sat panicked and immobile, those thoughts running in circles in my mind, Mama had writhed miserably on the floor.

"Go, Kathy!" she'd shouted through gritted teeth.

The panic in her voice had told me I had to do something. Squeezing my eyes shut, I'd summoned all the courage I'd had and I'd run into the kitchen to get the phone. The backdoor had still been open, but I'd ignored it and done exactly what Mama had said. When I'd hung up the phone, I'd tiptoed to the door and peeked out. There had been no sign of Johnny Ray or his truck. I'd closed and locked the door then returned to Mama's bedroom.

She had managed to prop herself up against the wall. With her eyes closed and her head tilted awkwardly to the side, she'd looked dead, and I'd panicked again. Easing nervously over to her, shaking with fear and cold for no reason as it was July, I'd leaned down close to her ear and whispered, "Mama."

She'd touched my leg and I'd nearly jumped out of my skin. "Ahhh---"

"Shhh. It's okay, baby," she'd whispered soothingly, without opening her eyes. The floor was wet where she had been laying and I'd stepped back.

"Mama," I'd said softly, "did you have an accident?"

"No, baby." She'd breathed deeply as if she had been in great pain. "My water broke that's all." Her voice was strained and tired. "Now, I need you to do a couple more things for me, okay?"

"Okay, Mama," I'd answered afraid of what they might be.

"I need you to wet a wash cloth with warm water and bring it to me. Then, I need you to get me a clean pair of panties and a nightgown."

Neither thing would take me too far from Mama, so I'd left to get them done as quickly as possible. Each time I'd glanced back at Mama she'd seemed closer to death. Even after she'd cleaned the blood from her face, her skin was red and bruised. I'd been terrified and hadn't known what to do to make things better, so I'd sat on the floor beside her until I'd heard the sirens and saw the lights flashing outside the bedroom window.

"Do you want me to help you up, Mama?" It was something I'd been doing for months and she'd looked like she'd needed it now more than ever.

"No, baby," she'd answered breathlessly. "Just go open the door, and show the men where I am."

CHAPTER EIGHT

Shouting brought my mind back into the hospital room where I'd spent the night in a chair beside Mama.

"Sophia," Aunt Grace implored, from the foot of the bed, "you can't get a black eye and busted lip from a fall. Someone did this to you and I want to know who!"

Mama studied her hands and I watched Johnny Ray. His eyes were fixed on Mama as if daring her to tell. I wanted to tell, to shout it right out, but I knew that would only upset Mama more and it just might set Johnny Ray off again. Instead, I stood helplessly by and watched as he got off scot free.

"I told you, I fell," Mama said so softly I wasn't sure if I had heard it or made it up.

"Damn it, Sophia, when are you going to take control of your life and stop letting low lifes like him treat you this way?"

I knew instantly that Aunt Grace had gone too far. Johnny Ray bowed up as if ready to hit her too. Anger flashed in Mama's eyes and she sat up in bed.

"What the hell do you know about my life, Ms. High and Mighty? You sit over there, way cross town, in your ivory tower and look down on people like me."

I eased back toward the door and watched Johnny Ray stick out his chest, stand a little straighter. He moved closer to Mama. It made me angry that he was encouraging Mama to attack Aunt Grace.

She obliged him. "I don't need you coming here telling me what to do. In fact, why don't you take your little card and teddy bear and get the hell out of my room."

Aunt Grace seemed on the verge of tears. "Sophia! You don't mean that."

"Like hell I don't."

"But we're sisters. I love you."

I wanted to hug Aunt Grace and tell her it would be alright in a day or two. But I stood rooted to the spot.

"When I need your kind of love, I'll let you know," Mama spat.

"That's right, baby," Johnny Ray said, putting his hand on Mama's shoulder. "You've got all the love you need right here." He tried to reach for me, but I moved closer to the door.

I couldn't believe he was saying that after what he'd done to her. I wanted to hit him myself. I wished Mama would push his hand away and tell Aunt Grace what had really happened.

But it was too late. When I looked up again, Aunt Grace was beside me. She hugged me tightly and whispered, "My telephone number is on this slip of paper." I felt her slide something into my back pocket. "Memorize it," she said, still holding on to me. "If you ever need anything, my sweet little niece, you call me. And I'll be there every time. Hang in there. *Her* life doesn't have to be *your* life." She kissed my cheek, then released me. Without a backward glance, Aunt Grace was gone.

CHAPTER NINE

"Kathy?" Aunt Grace whispered into the telephone as if a louder response might scare me away. "Is that you?" I exhaled, relieved that she remembered. "Yes ma'am," The lump that rose in my throat surprised me and made it difficult to speak. "It's me," I whispered. "Where are you? Are you alright?" Her concern was palatable and I wanted to assuage her fears.

"Yes, I'm alright," I said, but my voice cracked.

"Kathy, where are you sweetie? Has something happened?"

"Yes." A wall of emotion broke free and I sobbed into the receiver.

"Are you hurt, Kathy?" Aunt Grace asked calmly.

I sniffed hard, trying to compose myself. "No, I'm okay." The clerk handed me a napkin and I blew my nose. "I'm at a service station."

I heard her suck in a breath. "Oh, Kathy," she said calmly, "which service station? Can you tell me where you are?"

With the clerk's help, I gave Aunt Grace the information she needed. Then the clerk and I left the warmth of the glass case to make room for the new guy. We stood in front of the large glass doors, looking out onto the deserted parking lot.

"The streets are probably slick, so it might take her a while to get here," the clerk said. "But at least the sleeting has stopped."

I nodded. I was in no hurry to put Aunt Grace in the middle of the mess I'd made. The clerk and I stood together quietly for a minute.

"Well, it's time for me to head out." She studied my face. "You take care of yourself, Miss Kathy."

"I will," I assured her.

The clerk hugged me for a long time.

"Okay then," she said letting go but keeping her hands on my shoulders like the girl at the truck stop whose face I couldn't get out of my head. "Listen," she said. "Sometimes life can be cruel. It tries to break us. But stay strong, Miss Kathy. Believe in yourself and never let anyone steal your dreams." A tear ran down her cheek.

I felt sad for her and wondered if someone had stolen her dreams. She hugged me again, then said goodbye.

I watched her drive away in an old brown Chevrolet Chevet. Over time, a few other cars came and went; none of them were Aunt Grace. Then, a shiny black Mercedes Benz slowly pulled into the parking lot. I knew instantly who it was.

My hands resumed their shaking and my legs were suddenly too tired to hold me up. I was too weak to sustain my rapid heartbeat. My chest constricted and my mouth felt like cotton. As Aunt Grace was getting out of the car, I found it difficult to breath.

She looked the same, but different. Her short coffered dark brown curls were just as I remembered as was her caramel-colored face. She looked a lot like Mama did when she fixed herself up, only Aunt Grace's hair was shorter and she looked older and more sophisticated.

Aunt Grace saw me through the glass door and hesitated for a split second. Our eyes locked. Hers were lined at the edges and there was a look of concern etched into her face. She hurried through the door and pulled me into her arms. She smelled of expensive makeup and freshly ironed clothes.

"Oh, my sweet little niece," she said against the top of my head. She pushed me an arm's length away to get a look, and then pulled me back into her bosom. She did that a second time, and I felt compelled to remind her that I was alright.

We walked together, she with both of her arms around me, to the passenger side of the sleek black car. Aunt Grace opened the front door of the car for me and I climbed in. I breathed deeply inhaling the new car smell. The leather seats were gray and clean as was the black console with wood grain trim. I sank into the plush seat, leaned my head against the headrest, and closed my eyes. I was tired and relieved to finally feel safe.

Aunt Grace slid in gracefully, smiled at me, then pushed a button to crank the car. Whoa. I'd never seen anything like that before. Classical music filled the interior and I closed my eyes. I could feel her eyes on me. "Would you like to listen to something else?"

I jerked myself up afraid that my posture had given her the impression that I didn't like the music. "Oh, no, I like it. It's relaxing."

She patted my leg. "I'm glad. It's relaxing for me too; that's why I listen to it."

I eased back into the headrest and closed my eyes again. I wasn't ready to talk just yet and Aunt Grace seemed to sense it, because she didn't say anything else until she'd pulled the car into the garage of her house. I unbuckled my seatbelt and opened the car door. The garage smelled of fresh grass clippings and saw dust. I liked the scent of it.

It was a neat enough space. The Benz was parked on the right side near the door to the house. The walls had shelves and hooks that were lined with boxes and tools. A lawn mower was pushed onto one corner and a weed eater leaned in the opposite corner. A large green garbage can was just inside the garage door in the back left corner.

I followed Aunt Grace up two steps and into the house. We were in a laundry area and just ahead I could see the kitchen. The ivory-colored tile floor glistened in the light of the setting sun and the warmth of the house invited me farther inside. I turned around in wonder reminding myself to close my mouth as I followed her through the dining room with its cherry wood table for eight set for a dinner party, and into a spacious den, complete with a brick fireplace.

"Wow!" I said in awe of what I saw. "You live in a mansion!"

Aunt Grace chuckled nervously. "It's no mansion. But it is home."

"You live here by yourself?" I asked.

"I used to, but no, my husband, Cedric, lives here too."

"You're married? I didn't know that. Is he here?" I was standing in front of a bookcase that covered an entire wall. They had more books in this one room than our entire school library I thought.

"No, Cedric's in Arizona visiting his family. He left this morning, just before the weather turned bad. We've been married five years. I can't believe you didn't know that. Didn't your mother tell you about the wedding?"

"I don't think she got an invitation," I said, feeling the need to defend Mama.

"Of course she got an invitation. All of you were invited – Sophia, you, and Margaret Ann." She watched me for a minute as I pretended to read some of the book titles while trying to digest this new information. "How is Margaret Ann?"

"Mar Mar? She's fine."

"Mar Mar?"

"Yeah, that's what I call her sometimes."

Aunt Grace laughed.

"What?"

"That's funny. When we were girls, I used to call your mother So So."

"Really? So So?"

"Yeah, mostly because she was so, so annoying."

We both laughed at that.

"Why don't you take some of those clothes off Kathy? You look pretty uncomfortable."

I looked down, embarrassed. I did look rather foolish in three layers of clothes, but they were all that had kept me warm. Aunt Grace pointed down a hall to my left.

"The guest bedroom is down that hall – first door on the right."

CHAPTER TEN

The guest bedroom was about the size of the living room in our apartment, and its white carpet was fluffy and clean. I took off my shoes and rubbed my feet against the plush softness. I'd stepped out of a nightmare and into a fairytale complete with a full size canopied bed covered in pink linens, with matching white furniture. It seemed to be the kind of bedroom a princess would have.

I sat on the bed and tugged at my clothes. The first layer seemed to have fused with the one beneath. I worked so hard getting them off, sweat beads formed on my brow. As I struggled, I could hear Aunt Grace's voice. The pitch was an octave higher than moments before and her words were clipped. She was agitated. I strained to hear, but couldn't make out many of her words. There was something about the department of children's services and going to court, but most of it was mumbled. I worked harder to get undressed so I could come out and hear better.

Finally down to blue jeans and the pink sweater I'd gotten for Christmas, I folded the remainder of my clothes, sat them neatly on the dresser, and then pulled open the door.

"I said, I'll call you back later," I heard Aunt Grace say with quiet force, before hanging up the phone. Seeing me, she affixed a smile, which seemed strained.

"Was that about me?" I asked unable to stop myself.

"Yes, I'm afraid it was," she answered matter-of-factly.

Feeling guilty, I looked away.

"It was your mother."

"Mama?" My heart sank. I was sure that meant that she and Johnny Ray would be arriving any minute in his raggedy truck with smoke trailing from the tail pipe. "I'll get my stuff."

"Oh, I think that can wait," Aunt Grace said knowingly, letting go of the receiver. "Your mother was worried sick though, Kathy. She loves you very much, you know."

I averted my eyes. It wasn't that I didn't think Mama loved me. I just didn't think she cared about me, not really. Mama only cared about me to the extent that it was helpful to her. I meant nothing more to her than a servant does to his master.

"Kathy, sit with me." Aunt Grace said, patting the opposite cushion on the sofa. I sat crisscross applesauce leaning against the arm of the couch, prepared for a lecture.

"My sweet little niece," she began, touching my leg lightly. I liked the soft feel of her hand. "You've had a difficult childhood; and although I'm sure I don't know the half of it, it can't have been easy."

With the acknowledgement of my pain, fresh tears sprung to my eyes. Finally, someone understood. I felt the lump return to my throat, thick and burning. But I refused to cry.

"Your mother has said and done things she probably shouldn't have. And those things have hurt you very deeply."

I nodded, fighting back tears.

"I'm equally certain that she's terribly sorry for them, Kathy, because you see, her childhood – and mine – weren't that different from yours.

Yeah right, I thought, and folded my arms across my chest with a humph.

"Our parents, your grandparents, split up when we were in elementary school. Things at home were unstable for years before Father left, but they got a lot worse afterwards."

Aunt Grace got up from the couch. "Come help me put on dinner."

CHAPTER ELEVEN

"After our father left," Aunt Grace began, picking up a potato to peel, "Mother was not the same person. She started having fun for the first time in a long time. Instead of being quiet and nervous, she would hum tunes and smile a funny-looking grin. She didn't sit alone on the front porch anymore; there was always someone with her. Suddenly, Mother had friends. They would be with her when we left for school in the mornings and they'd still be there when we returned in the afternoon, after having just been at our house late the night before.

"Her mother, our Grandma Thompson, did not like this new version of Mother and Sophia and I became fiercely protective of her. Mother was a sweet person who, we surmised, just wanted to feel good and be happy. Unfortunately, it seemed that there were a lot of people taking advantage of her generous spirit.

"To keep Grandma Thompson from knowing too much about what was going on with our mother, each morning Sophia and I would pick up the empty bottles, wash the cups, and make our bed before leaving for school. I would keep up with everyone's laundry, putting the dirty clothes in an old pillowcase and folding and stacking the clean ones. On Saturdays, I would carry the pillowcase to

Grandma's house to wash, careful to use only one cup of her Tide Laundry Detergent.

"Deep down, Grandma wanted Mother to be happy too. Some Saturday mornings, she would press a ten-dollar bill into my hand to give to Mother. I was very careful not to lose it because I knew how much we needed the money. Often, it meant Mother could buy dinner for us that week. But sometimes it meant she and her friends could have a really big party and that was the part that bothered Grandma Thompson the most.

"At the parties, someone would usually bring a radio to play music. The grown-ups would sing and dance with the music. Some of them would couple up and kiss to the slow songs. Basie, as in Count Basie, because of his knowledge about jazz music, had become a regular visitor and would always couple up with Mother. Why Mother would let him kiss her was a mystery to me. He was as mean as a snake and was rough with her. He called it playing around, but Sophia and I didn't like it.

"It was particularly disturbing to wake up after one of these parties to find Basie still in the house. "Doesn't he have a home of his own to go to," we'd whisper between ourselves. I was able to ignore him, but he had decided to make Sophia his personal servant. For some reason Mr. Basie, as were forced to call him 'out of respect', believed that if he needed a thing, Sophia should be the one to fetch it. "Bring my shoes…Fix me a drink…Not too much juice…Pick up this…Get me that… She told me that she was scared of him and I tried to protect her the best I could, but I was only a child myself."

Aunt Grace's voice cracked a bit and she turned to put the chicken in the oven. I watched her back imagining a pained expression on her face. She was telling me a lot of things that would have been hard for me to talk about. I felt sorry for Aunt Grace and wished I could do something to make her feel better.

Aunt Grace busied herself at the stove, then turned toward me. But instead of making eye contact, she looked at the blinds behind me as if a movie was projected on them. "After school he'd tell everyone to go outside, except Sophia," Aunt Grace continued. "He'd say things like, 'You didn't make my bed before you left.' Of course, he would have still been in it, but that hadn't mattered. She'd have to stay inside to do it. When I came back inside, she'd be crying. I could never get her to tell me what had happened; I just knew it had to have been bad.

"So, while he and Mother drank the afternoon and evening away, Sophia was stuck in the house. Mr. Basie was especially picky about the way *his* room was done. He wanted *his* bed made with hospital corners so that his feet didn't get cold at night. Mother never said a word. I think she was afraid too. Of course, having seen his wicked scowls first hand, I could understand why.

"After a few months, Mr. Basie was more than a regular; he had moved in. Although Mother described him as the 'man of the house', he was far from a father. He didn't want any more to do with us than we wanted to do with him, except Sophia. He wanted her at his beck and call. If he became angry with one of us, Mother would hear about it. He'd yell and curse something awful. He would rarely strike one of us, but I had a feeling Mother had been on the receiving end of his anger more than a few times."

I cringed, having seen my own mama go through the same thing at the hands of Johnny Ray.

"Like she'd been with Father, whom we hadn't seen in a couple of years, Mother had once again become withdrawn. People stopped coming around. Mother was nervous, always fussing over Mr. Basie, making sure he was happy. He should've been. He was living with us, not working, and getting all the food he wanted and all the liquor he could drink. What more could he want, I used to wonder. Then I found out that what he really wanted; and it was more than any man should've had."

CHAPTER TWELVE

Aunt Grace began pulling serving dishes, plates, glasses, and silverware from various cabinets and drawers. I helped her carry them into the dining room where we set the long formal table for just the two of us.

For a time, we worked in thoughtful silence. I was trying to digest what she'd told me so far, but my gut told me there was more. When she spoke again, it was softly as if she was far away. I stopped moving to hear her better.

"One day after giving Mother the ten-dollar bill from Grandma Thompson, she asked me to go to the store with her. Sophia asked if she could go too, but Mr. Basie said that he needed Sophia to stay home to help take care of him. The way he said it made the hair on my neck stand up and Sophia started to cry. I begged Mother to take Sophia with us, but she just snatched my hand and walked off.

"Sophia hollered for us not to leave her and Mr. Basie yelled at her to shut up. She didn't and I heard her even after I could no longer see the house. I knew something terrible was going to happen. I could feel it with every fiber of my being. I urged Mother to go back, but she kept walking forward seemingly more determined than ever to get to the store.

"It was a hot day and sweat ran down my face and chest, but I walked as fast as I could back to the house. It was eerily quiet and the porch was deserted. I thought for a moment that Mr. Basie had finally left. My heart skipped a beat.

"But inside the house was a different story. Mr. Basie was slouched across the sofa with his shirt unbuttoned and his socked feet spread wide apart. He was picking his teeth and sweating. He smelled horribly. I ran past him looking for Sophia. The covers of the bottom bunk were strewn everywhere and I found my sister lying in the fetal position of the bottom bunk, silent and shaking uncontrollably.

"I got on my knees and scooted as close to the bed as I could. I wrapped my arms around her and hummed *Jesus Loves Me* until she stopped shaking. I told her I'd get Mother for her, but she clung to me, not letting me leave. So, we sat like that until Mother came looking for us."

"Sophia whispered the things that had happened while we'd been gone. She told Mother how Mr. Basie had forced himself on her. She told Mother that she'd tried to fight him off, but that he'd hit her and held her down despite her struggles. Mother grew angrier with each word and I was sure she'd finally stand up to Mr. Basie and throw him out."

"When Sophia finished, Mother slapped her hard across that face and shouted that she was a liar. Sophia crumbled into the fetal position and began rocking herself. Mother yelled for her to stop it. I sat in shock, unable to move."

"Suddenly, Mother stood up and left the room. She returned seconds later with Mr. Basie behind her. She told him what Sophia had said. Sophia covered her face with her hands and trembled violently. Mr. Basie stomped and cursed and threatened for a long time and then he snatched off his belt and began hitting Sophia with it. I grabbed his arm and he slung me hard to the floor. I got up again and started hitting him in the back shouting for him to leave Sophia alone."

"Mother grabbed me and dragged me kicking and clawing out of the room. She held me down on the same sofa Mr. Basie had been draped across minutes earlier. Sophia's screams reverberated through the house for an eternity until finally Mr. Basie was too tired to hit her anymore. As he came into the room disheveled and stinking, Mother let me up."

"I ran in to comfort Sophia, and found her nearly unconscious on the floor. She was bleeding badly." Aunt Grace was crying openly. "I did what I could to clean her up," Aunt Grace sobbed, "but it was as if she was a torn rag doll that needed to sewn back together. She missed a week of school and I cried every morning that I was forced to go without her."

"After that, Mr. Basie grew even more violent, especially toward Mother. They'd drink hard, and then fight hard. Mr. Basie would sometimes have scratch marks across his face, but Mother was more often bruised and sometime bloodied. Then, one day when I was 13 and Sophia was 10, we came home and found Mother on the floor of the living room. She wasn't breathing."

"We ran to Grandma Thompson's house and that was the last day Sophia and I spent together. Father's sister, Aunt Victoria, came for me and Grandma Thompson kept Sophia. Three miles might not seem like far, but for us, it was worlds away. Sophia was separated from everyone she knew. We attended different schools and Father's family was no longer speaking to Mother's family, so there was no way for Sophia and me to see one another."

"Of course I heard stories and rumors about Sophia – from clubs to drugs to things even more terrible – but I wasn't ready to believe any of it – not about my sister. All

I knew for sure was that she'd had some trouble and dropped out of school. I finished high school, and was quickly sent away to college. When I returned to Memphis, I tried to find Sophia, but no one knew exactly where she was. "

"After that we'd run into each other from time to time, but we'd always lose contact. My sister didn't stay in one place very long."

Aunt Grace looked up at me. My tears flowed silently, some pooling beneath my nose, others dripping onto the tablecloth. She put her arms around me and we rocked there together still standing beside the dining room table. "As I said earlier, your mom has had a very difficult life. She never had a good role model for motherhood. In fact, she never had a positive role model of any sort. She has done – and is doing – for you and Margaret Ann, the best she can. While I don't agree with many of the decisions she's made – especially those concerning you – I do ask that you cut your mom some slack."

I nodded, unable to speak.

"Are you alright?" she asked, her breath against my hair.

I nodded again.

"I've given you a lot of information tonight, haven't I, sweetie?"

"Um hmm."

"Do you have any questions?"

I closed my eyes and pulled in a deep breath. "Just one."

"Okay---"

"Do you know who my daddy is?"

'No, Kathy, I'm afraid I don't."

I let out the breath I didn't know I'd been holding in. It had been a long shot, but some part of me hoped Aunt Grace would know. We sat in silence for a while more. "So, what happens to me now?" I asked.

"Tomorrow morning, I take you home."

I studied the flowers in the area rug. "Thanks for coming to get me, Aunt Grace."

"You're welcome, Kathy. I told you – anytime you need me, I'll be there."

CHAPTER THIRTEEN

The drive home was difficult. Yesterday's ice had turned to dirty slush and the ugly frozen water seemed to run through my veins. I shivered. Nervous about what would come next, I couldn't seem to rein in my scattered thoughts. How would Mama respond to seeing me? Would she be waiting at the door with one of Johnny Ray's belts behind her back? Would she hit me in front of Aunt Grace? How would she react to having Aunt Grace in the apartment? I closed my eyes, trying to shut out the impending doom flooding my mind.

Mama was waiting at the door, hands on her hips, lips pursed.

"Hey Mama," I said softly, searching her face for clues about her mood, her intentions.

"Kathy," she answered cooly, averting her eyes and stepping aside to let me in.

The house was oddly quiet and free of the children Mama babysat each day. There were usually six to ten kids running around the house on any given day. They ranged in age from newborn to grade school, coming and going haphazardly depending on their parents' work schedules and the school bus drop off times. Mama fed them breakfast, lunch and sometimes dinner. In return, she received $25 a week per child. Less if there were siblings.

With all the kids being out for the holiday, the apartment should be full.

I turned to ask Mama where everyone was and saw her standing toe to toe, a couple of inches above Aunt Grace. Neither said anything at first. Then Aunt Grace attempted to hug Mama. Mama shifted out of the way.

Aunt Grace let her arms fall to her side. "It's good to see you, Sophia."

"Humph," Mama answered, rolling her eyes.

My stomach fluttered. I hoped Mama wouldn't be too harsh with Aunt Grace. I tried to think of something to say to break the ice, but since I was the cause of the trouble, I couldn't.

"May I come in?" Aunt Grace asked.

"May as well; you're here."

I breathed a sign of relief.

"Don't be too angry with her," Aunt Grace said softly after a while.

"So now you want to tell me how to raise her too?"

"No, Sophia, you seem to be doing a fine job all by yourself." Her sarcasm wasn't lost on Mama.

"Look, I promised not to beat the hell out of her," Mama said flicking her cigarette in my general direction. "I didn't say anything about you."

Aunt Grace's face hardened. "I'm trying to keep this civil, Sophia. I returned Kathy as I said I would. Now you hold up your end of the bargain."

"Fine," Mama said nastily. "But all scheduling goes through me. There'll be none of you just showing up whenever you damn well please."

Showing up, I thought excitedly. I almost grinned in spite of fearing for my life. My eyes went from Mama to Aunt Grace back to Mama.

"I'll call to arrange any visits far in advance."

"And no more than once a month," Mama said blowing smoke into her face.

"No more."

"Fine."

"Great. I'll call you," she said brightly.

"Great," Mama repeated, mimicking her. "You do that." Mama speared the cigarette butt into an empty Coke can.

"Bye, Kathy," Aunt Grace said from just inside the door. "Take care of yourself."

Afraid to move, lest I push my luck, I said goodbye from the opposite side of the kitchen.

* * *

The school bell rang and startled me from my thoughts. I'd gotten lost in time again the way I sometimes did when I was bored. And it couldn't get more boring than Mr. Alton and chemistry. They were a lethal combination.

Fortunately, the next class was English, my favorite subject. Tenth grade English had been okay, even though it was a little heavy on the grammar. This year though, it was all about reading. From Shakespeare to Edgar Alan Poe to Sylvia Plath, I liked it all. Although, it was still hard to fit in homework time, I found a way to finish my studying while watching the kids. I read the stories, plays and poems out loud to them – all except Poe. His writing was way too scary for kids.

I didn't want to write like him. I didn't want to write like Shakespeare either. My writing was more like Sylvia Plath. I loved to write about real things that were happening in our neighborhood and in our school. When my friends read my stories they said it was as if someone understood what they were going through. They would pass pages of my stories around the lunch table and talk about the characters and their situations like they were real people. Hearing them talk about my stories made me feel like I mattered.

"Have you seen this?" Jonetta asked, interrupting my thoughts. She flashed a royal blue sheet of paper.

"No, what is it?" I reached for the flyer. At nearly six feet tall, she was a full head above me. At moments like these, her height was so annoying.

"An announcement," she said laughing at her own coyness, lowering her arms.

"What kind of announcement? Give it to me." I snatched the sheet away.

SCHOOL-WIDE ESSAY WRITING CONTEST was in big letters across the top. I stopped so quickly, Jonetta nearly plowed over me.

"I thought that might get your attention," she said standing behind me. "See," Jonetta pointed over my shoulder, "the topic is *The Greatest Challenge of My Life.* You certainly have enough of those."

I whirled around, "What's that supposed to mean?"

"You know exactly what it means," she answered, shoving me into the classroom. We took our seats next to Pete and Richard who were already talking about the contest.

"Are you going to enter?"

"I don't know," I said. "I just heard about it."

"You should," Richard encouraged.

"Yeah, you're the best writer we know," Pete added.

The bell rang, and we looked up to see Mrs. Scott perched on the edge of her desk holding a copy of the same flyer.

CHAPTER FOURTEEN

The boys loved to watch Mrs. Scott. She had shapely legs and wore flouncing skirts that brushed just below the knee, drawing everyone's eyes to her muscular calves and high- heels. They talked about her perky breasts and round butt as if they were works of art. The fact that she gave none of them the time of day only added to her attractiveness. I liked her because she was smart and always had a come back for the wise guys. She knew how to set them straight and sound intelligent doing it.

Perched on the right side of her desk, legs crossed beneath a pink skirt and white peep-toe heels that showed off hot pink nail polish, Mrs. Scott smiled out at the class. I watched attentively, but her eyes settled on Amy when she spoke.

"I have exciting news for the class." Her straight sparkly teeth shone through a glossy smile. "The English Department is holding a school-wide essay writing contest."

An excited murmur rose in the classroom filled with honor students as everyone turned to talk to someone else.

"Some of you are very strong writers," she continued, nodding at Heather and locking eyes again with Amy. They sat taller in their chairs and I slouched for spite. Heather and Amy were the bane of my school-day existence. They had picked on me since seventh grade. You'd think they'd be bored with it by now and move on. But no, that was not the case.

"The topic, *The Greatest Challenge of My Life*, should provide you with plenty of leeway to take the essay any direction you choose. We're interested in life as you've experienced it, so the essays can be written in first person. That will also make them easier for you to read."

"Read?" I asked aloud without thinking.

"Yes. The winner will read their essay at the year-end awards program."

That was an unexpected twist.

A hand shot up from the back. "Yes, Zoe?" We all turned around.

"What's the prize?"

"The satisfaction of being identified as the best writer in the school," Mrs. Scott answered matter-of-factly.

Some of the kids moaned.

"That's all?" a person near the door asked smartly.

"That… and a $50 gift certificate to the mall."

The murmur grew to a roar. Mrs. Scott savored the moment and allowed it to continue for some time. I became lost in my thoughts. I wanted to win the contest. There wasn't much that I was good at, but the one thing I knew I could do well, was write.

I wrote as often as I could – about Mama; all those annoying kids she babysat; my dream of leaving home and never coming back; thoughts of being a successful newspaper columnist, sipping wine with my girlfriends in exotic places all over the world with no men and *no kids*. But all of those were just private thoughts put in a notebook that I kept under my mattress and pushed to the very middle so that even if someone was looking they wouldn't easily find it.

This essay contest was different. This time I wanted to write about something important, the one thing in the world I could make no sense of, the thing that bothered me most: not having a father.

My father was non-existent. He'd never been seen and was never mentioned. About the time I started middle school, I became aware that this was not the norm. Everyone seemed to have a daddy. Even if he didn't live with them, they at least knew him.

All of my friends had fathers. Cynthia's dad was out of work, but he walked her to the bus stop every morning and was there again in the afternoon to walk her home. Daphne's dad sat on a bench near the playground with a brown paper bag, but he left us pretty much alone. And even though Shane's father was in jail, he wrote letters to his son. I knew because Shane had shown one to me the year before when we'd been the only ones at the pool.

By the time I started seventh grade, the fact that I didn't have a father had become common knowledge and Heather and Amy took great pleasure in letting me know it. I was thinking about it after biology class the day we'd been covering hereditary traits. I knew about recessive traits and dominant traits. I could calculate the likelihood of eye color and facial features based on those of the parents and grandparents. I was so interested in how it all worked that I made the only perfect score on the test. I smiled as I walked down the hall.

"She thinks she's special because she looks different," Heather said to Amy loud enough for me to hear.

"Yeah," Amy answered. "Like she's an *Island Girl* or something."

My smile vanished.

"But she isn't; is she?"

"Nope."

"Nope. She's just some off-brand, half-breed." Heather said nastily.

"Yep." they said in unison. "Just an off-brand, half-breed."

My heart raced. I knew what was coming. I walked faster trying to put distance between me and them. But they picked up their pace as well.

"I'll bet *she* doesn't even know what she is," Heather answered. "Hey!" she shouted, her red sweater catching up to me. "What *are* you, anyway?" she sneered, knocking the books from my arms and sprinting past me.

Both girls laughed as my papers tumbled out and scattered across the hallway. Everyone turned to see the commotion, but no one stopped to help. I noticed one boy pause and seemed to look concerned, but I was too embarrassed to make eye contact. Instead, I took my time gathering and stacking my things, trying to allow the crowd to disburse before standing up.

Careful not to make a sound, I shouted at Heather and Amy in my head, "Why do you hate me? You don't even know me!"

Breathing deeply, I composed myself and picked up my stuff off the floor. Holding everything close to my chest, I walked as fast as I could toward the line of big yellow school busses, looking for number 1986. My bus was all the way at the front of the line and about to pull away. I ran for it. Books and papers bounced dangerously. Jeers and taunts rang in my ears.

I pretended to ignore them, but how could I really? What was so wrong with me? My chestnut colored curls were thick, but not unmanageable. I was just barely a shade too dark to be called olive-skinned, more like a mocha latte with extra milk. Maybe I was a little thick, but there were bigger girls – even in their clicque. Why did they have to hate me?

Breathing hard, I could hear the whispers as I climbed onto the bus. All the seats were taken, except the one next to a boy everyone called Peabody. Rumors were that his mom was an alcoholic and did nothing to take care of him or his little brother – apparently including never doing laundry. But it didn't matter; they teased him as if it was somehow his own fault. Craning my neck for another option, I jumped when the bus driver shouted, "Sit down already!"

The bus erupted with laughter.

I smiled weakly at Peabody and he slid over. "Thanks," I mumbled. Leaning back against the seat, I tried to relax. But the smell was overwhelming. Making an effort to be inconspicuous, I put my hand across my nose and pretended to wipe it. Just as I exhaled, the bus lurched forward unexpectedly causing my books to slide off my lap. "Agh!" Panic stricken, my body seemed to move in slow motion.

Before I could do anything, Peabody reached out his hand to stop the impending disaster. "Thanks," I said again, this time with a genuine smile.

As the bus groaned forward, Peabody nodded and turned to look out the window beside him. With my right hand still covering my nose, I stared past Peabody, through the same window, and watched until the bus approached my stop.

"See you later," I said standing up.

He said nothing.

Although that was four years ago, the day stood out in my mind and served as a painful reminder of just how difficult life is when you look different from everyone around you and no one can or will tell you why. High school students didn't have the luxury of riding school buses. Those who didn't have their own transportation had to walk. Other kids walked together through the apartment complex in couples or groups, talking and giggling. Walking alone, I wondered if they were talking about me. Self-consciously, I adjusted my clothes and hurried my pace. Ignoring them, I focused my mind on the essay contest.

"Hey Mama," I said coming through the door.

"Kathy! Kathy! You're home," Margaret Ann cried, running at me full speed.

"Umph ---" She hit with a thud, temporarily knocking the wind out of me. Recovering quickly, I wrapped my arms around her thin seven-year-old frame, then picked her up and twirled her around.

"Wheeee!"

I smiled into my little sister's face then returned her feet to the brown, threadbare carpet.

"Again!" she squealed.

Again I twirled her. With Margaret Ann still in mid-air, I called, "Mama?"

"Hmm?"

"There's an essay contest at school." I lowered Margaret Ann and looked at Mama.

"Yeah...And..."

"Well, I'm entering it."

"For what?"

"I just want to."

She didn't respond.

"Anyway, Mama, they're going to announce the winner at the year-end awards program."

"And?"

"And I thought you might want to come."

"To the school," she snorted. "Why would I want to do that?"

"Because I might win," I said quietly, a lot less sure than I had been moments ago.

"*You* might win? Humph."

I shrugged and pried myself away from Margaret Ann who was still wobbling against my legs. She followed me into the bedroom.

"Spin me again," she asked.

"Not right now, Mar Mar."

"Yes, now. Spin me!"

"Not now," I said patting her head.

"Spin me, Kathy," she whined.

"No Mar Mar." She never knew when to stop.

"Mama! Kathy won't spin me!" she shouted down the hall.

"Margaret Ann," I said angrily. "Why'd you do that?"

"Kathy!" Mama shouted back. "Spin that baby!"

"See. Now you've gotten Mama mad at me."

"Well, I told you to spin me," she answered defiantly, hands on her hips looking like a tiny version of Mama.

I turned away, sat at the foot of my bed, and folded my arms refusing to do anything more.

"Mama! Kathy still won't spin me!"

"Kathy!" Mama yelled.

I leaned in close to Margaret Ann's face, "You make me sick," I said nastily. I grabbed her arm hard. When I looked into her face, her eyes were sad and when I put her down she didn't ask for another turn.

I flopped back onto my bed and stared into the pealing ceiling thinking again about the essay. I didn't care what Mama thought. I could win the contest. I was a good writer. I had never really talked about my dad with anyone before. Whenever anyone asked me about him, I would make up some extravagant story to explain his absence.

In second grade when John Fleming asked me about my dad, I said he was French. In my mind, he was a handsome, generous man who lived in a *château* near a peaceful village by the sea. That theory changed when I learned about the Vietnam War in fifth grade. That's when I imagined him as a captain in the Marines who had died heroically saving his comrades during battle. Later, he was a sheik from Arabia. With my hair texture and kind of olive skin, I could pull that off.

Margaret Ann walked over. "What are you thinking about?"

On the verge of tears, I turned my head. I could never form words when my emotions were this close to the surface.

"What's wrong, Kathy?" She asked, stroking my arm. "Are you mad at me?"

I closed my eyes and composed myself. After a minute I was able to answer. "No, I'm not mad at you Mar Mar. I'm okay." I made an effort to lighten my mood. "Are you ready for your bath? I'll run the water for you."

"Yay! Do we have bubbles?"

I got up and took her by the hand. Once Mama and Johnny Ray closed the door to their room, they were not to be disturbed. It was my job to get Margaret Ann ready for bed each night. In the mornings, I combed her hair and got her dressed for school, but because I left for the bus stop before Margaret Ann, when the door closed behind me, she became Mama's responsibility.

Long after Margaret Ann was curled into a knot around her pillow and breathing deeply I lay in bed trying to figure out how to write my essay. I cried hot angry tears that burned my throat, but I was quiet, making sure not to wake my little sister and thus invite the wrath of Mama if she had to come in to settle Margaret Ann back down.

A girl misses a lot when she doesn't have a father. It's intangible, but there's susceptibility, an element of instability born of the longing for unconditional male approval. It was affecting me already, and I wasn't yet fully aware of just how profoundly.

The sound of the door to Mama's room opening gave me a start and I instantly stopped crying. I snatched the covers over my head and lay perfectly still, forcing myself to breathe slowly as the footsteps grew closer. I wished again that our door had a lock on it, but Mama couldn't stand secrets and she thought that a lock on my bedroom door would allow me to keep things from her.

I could hear his shallow raspy breaths getting closer and my own breath caught in my throat. I fought back the urge to cough. When his ashen, calloused feet were beside my bed, it was as if I could feel their clamminess on me. I cringed. I could almost see him standing there, his face the color of dust with short curly hair a shade of orange like Mississippi Delta clay. My fists were clinched so tightly my hands began to cramp. I prayed silently that he would leave as quickly as he had appeared.

"Kathy," he whispered standing over me.

Don't you dare move, I willed to myself.

"Kathy, you sleep?"

My breathing stopped altogether, but my heartbeat was so loud, I was sure he could hear it.

"Johnny Ray," Mama called. "You in the bathroom?"

He tiptoed backwards and tried to throw his voice, "Uh…Yeah."

"Hurry up and come back to bed, baby. It's getting cold in here."

For the longest time, everything was still and silent. I didn't dare so much as exhale. Finally, his feet shifted and his rasping breath faded away.

"Thank you, Jesus," I whispered into the darkness.

CHAPTER FIFTEEN

I spent all of the following day trying to get Johnny Ray out of my head. He was scary enough as himself, but when he'd been drinking, he was volatile, dictatorial, and downright mean. I did my best to stay out of his way as a general rule and to be nearly invisible when alcohol was anywhere around. How I wished my own dad was in my life. After school, I focused that energy on the essay.

Lost in thought, I felt myself miss the curb, tried to grab something to hold onto, but caught only air and went down hard, face-first into the street, sending everything flying. Why was I always such a klutz? The feeling of ineptitude brought tears to my eyes. My mind was a jumble of frustrations. I hurt everywhere, but the most agonizing was the knot in my stomach.

If I were honest, at the heart of my pain, the aching in the very depths of my soul was the thought that I was the reason my father had left, that I had not been enough of a reason for him to stay, that I had in some way not measured up. I craved knowledge of who he was and why he had left me to fend for myself. I was desperate for a love that would be meant just for me. I longed to have a father to protect me, to tell me I was special, to sooth my fears, and to threaten those who said and did hurtful things to me. I wanted a father to rescue me from the mess of a life Mama had created.

All the insecurities, all the hurt feelings, all my anxieties bubbled up to the surface and spilled out in anguished sobs. Hurrying home, I found the resolve I needed and decided that this was the day I'd confront Mama and discover the truth. I sniffed hard and wiped my eyes with the sleeve of my shirt, growing angrier and bolder with each step. Bursting through the back door, I found Mama sitting at the kitchen table in her faded pink housecoat with a Filter King Kool cigarette in one hand, fondling a can of Coke with the other. The kids were sitting in front of the television enthralled with Sesame Street. Mama was staring out the window, but turned toward the door when I came in.

"What in the world happened to you?" she asked taking the wind out of my sails.

"Ma'am?"

"What happened? Your clothes are all over the place. Your face is scarred and red. Your knee is bleeding. And your papers are everywhere?"

I looked down at myself. "Oh." I hadn't noticed that my knee was bleeding. Suddenly it throbbed. "I fell."

"Aw, Baby. Come here and let me look at you."

I walked gingerly over to her, now conscious of the pain.

"Oh, Kathy, you've been crying." Her scrunched up face looked like she was the one in pain. She took my cheeks in her broad hands and wiped the remnants of tears with her thumbs. "What's the matter, baby?"

I wasn't prepared for kindness from her – that energy was usually spent on Margaret Ann. The lump that appeared in my throat made it hard to breathe. This rare show of tenderness toward me brought fresh tears and, surprisingly, Mama was quick to comfort me. I put my books down on the table and collapsed into her lap. She put her arms around me and gently swayed.

"Tell Mama what's wrong?" she soothed.

The words spilled out fast and furiously as I told her about the mean girls, their shrill laughter, the comments about me and my ethnicity, and how much I wanted to know who my father was. With this last declaration, Mama's arms went rigid. The gentle rocking stopped. I lifted my head to see her face. There was a far off look in her eyes as she gazed out the window again.

"Mama, who is my father?"

"Johnny Ray is your daddy, girl."

"No, Mama," I said, my frustration getting the best of me. "That's Margaret Ann's father. I'm talking about my *real* father."

"Johnny Ray is as real as it gets around here. He's the one who puts food on the table. He's the only *father* you've ever known and he's the only one you're ever gonna know."

"But I need to..."

"Need to what?" Her words were a flash of lightening, quick and harsh. She was angry and I knew it, but I couldn't stop myself. She took a long drag on her cigarette and blew the smoke through her nose.

"I need to know who my real father is so I can know who I am."

"What do you mean, so you can know who you are?" She almost laughed. "You're my daughter. You're a beautiful, smart girl, Kathy. And who your daddy is ain't got nothing to do with that."

I'd never heard her compliment me before. She'd never said that I was pretty or smart. But I couldn't let that distract me. This was more important. "That's not what I'm talking about," I pressed.

"Then just what are you talking about?" she spat, pushing me off her lap and standing up.

From the floor, I watched her walk over to the sink, smoke streaming in her wake. I pulled myself up to sit in the chair still warm from her heat. "I'm just...I just want to know what color I am."

"You're black," she said without turning from the window.

"I'm not black," I shouted back, then, closed my eyes tightly and waited for her to come back and smack me.

She didn't. Instead she sighed loudly. It was more like a moan really. I had pushed too hard and hurt her feelings. My heart pounded, and I was flooded with a guilt that had become all too familiar. I remembered Aunt Grace's words. Mine was a good mother, doing the best she could to keep the lights on, food on the table, and us in a place at least one step above public housing. I knew that I needed to stop being so difficult, but the urgent question was unrelenting. It rang in my ears, pushing the guilt aside.

"Mama," I ventured more tentatively, making my voice as soft and apologetic as I could. "Will you at least tell me what color he is?"

She sucked hard on the cigarette and glared at me. I sat still and waited.

"I don't remember," she finally said with the type of sigh a person lets out after giving up on a struggle. Her unexpected words hung in the air for an eternity. I was waiting for an explanation and simultaneously trying to understand the information I'd just gotten.

"How can you not remember?"

"I just can't."

"Well, what did he look like?"

"I don't know what he looked like."

"What do you mean you don't know what he looked like? What exactly do you remember?" I pushed.

"Nothing! I don't know who your father is," she shouted through clenched teeth. Her eyes had hardened into tiny beads.

It wasn't the harshness of her words or the pained look on her face that made me shrink away from Mama and against the wall. It was her words. She didn't know *who* my father was.

"How can you make a baby and not know who the father is?"

"Don't you dare sit there and pass judgment on me, Kathleen Sumner!"

I looked at the floor helplessly.

"You don't know what it was like back then. I was living hand to mouth, staying with this person and that. I paid my way with whatever I had. Sometime it was money and sometimes it wasn't."

She paused to light another cigarette and take a drag. I studied the crumbs on the kitchen floor. I had the urge to get the broom and sweep.

"All you need to know is that when you came along all that changed." She sucked in, flicked an ash into the sink, blew out, and came over to me. I slid back down onto the floor and she took her seat at the kitchen table. I leaned against her leg and she stroked my hair.

"I loved you the minute I knew you were in me. And I straightened right up. I got a job at the Waffle House and moved into a shelter. After you were born, the government helped me get an apartment. It was the first time I'd had a real home since my own mama died. And I did that for you."

Her voice cracked. "Everything I do, Kathy, is for you – and Margaret Ann. You kids are my life." She wiped a tear from her right eye and sipped from the warm Coke can. I hugged her leg and let my own tears flow unchecked. This was the closest I'd ever felt to my mama and I wanted it to last forever.

"For your whole life, I've been both your mama and your daddy. Anybody can make a baby, Kathy. A real man stays and pays the bills. Johnny Ray may not have made you, but he helps take care of you. So, you don't have to ask me who your daddy is any more. Just look around and see who's here."

"And as to what color you are," she said snuffing out her cigarette. "You're black like me and your grandmother before me. She could've passed for white, but she didn't. She chose to be what her family was, and she was proud of it. That's what you are, Kathy – black. And don't you ever forget it."

With that, she pushed herself up, picked up her pack of cigarettes, and left me and the kitchen.

CHAPTER SIXTEEN

As the semester wore on, things at school grew hectic, with the scheduling of our senior pictures, attending college fairs, and studying for the ACT and SAT. Our junior year was wrapping up and my friends and I were excited about becoming seniors. At the year-end awards program, which marked the official last day of the senior class, the winner of the essay contest would be announced. All of this had me thinking about how I'd even gotten this far. I never would have made it without my friends: Jonetta, Richard, and Pete.

Jonetta was my best friend. A brilliant, smart-mouth, dark chocolate girl, she had a beautiful face, despite a three inch scar on its left side. The wound, which looked remarkably like railroad tracks, began at the tip of her eye and formed a crescent moon around to her cheek. She was a power forward on the girls' basketball team.

The fact that Jonetta was tall, muscular and loud intimidated most people, making them avoid her. But there was something about her that drew me to her. Maybe it was because she was bolder than I would ever be. I admired that about her. It wasn't until much later that I learned she'd lost her own mother when she was in third grade. That made me cry. I certainly felt cheated for not having a father, but losing a mother had to be twice as hard.

She definitely had it worse than me. We were best friends from that day on.

Jonetta lived in the apartment complex north of ours, so we sometimes walked to and from school together. But today she had a basketball team meeting. I was on my own and rather enjoyed the mile-long walk home. I loved springtime: flowers bloomed and grass grew to cover brown patchy lawns, scents were fresh and sweet, and the days held a sense of hope for what might come. Today, the air was warm and the sky was a brilliant blue, without a single cloud. I soaked in the solitude; it gave me time to think about the essay. I was growing nervous about it. Writing my story for teachers to read was one thing. Reading it aloud before the entire student body was something else altogether. Everyone would then know the truth about my father – that I didn't have one – and that thought scared me. The last thing I needed was more people teasing me. But it would also be freeing in some ways. I could stop pretending to be normal and finally be myself.

My thoughts drifted to Mama. Every day after school, my first task was to walk to the store to pick-up whatever grocery items she needed. Mama didn't have a car, and Johnny Ray wasn't about to use his gas to go to the store for a few measly items. The only time he took us grocery shopping was when the food stamp card was activated. That's because there were too many bags to carry and he could put whatever he wanted into the grocery cart. His favorites went in first; he was the man of the house after all. Other things came and went depending on how much money Mama had during a certain month.

Back home from my afternoon trip to the store, I'd have to change all the kids' diapers, and then take them outside to play so Mama could have a break and cook dinner. She'd call us in when it was time to eat and I'd help her feed the kids, including Margaret Ann.

Most of the children left between 5:30 and 6:00 each evening. But there were always one or two whose parents were late. We worked around them. Mama and I divided the cleaning into various rooms, and when I finished my rooms I was allowed to do my homework, which Mama thought was a complete waste of time. After homework, I had to get Margaret Ann bathed and ready for bed.

Because I had to help with the children, but mostly because Mama didn't trust me to be out of her sight for one second, I didn't participate in extracurricular activities or attend any after school games or dances. I didn't have a cell phone and didn't dare give anyone her phone number.

It wasn't too much of a problem though. My friends understood that things were different for me. I'm not sure how we maintained a friendship given how little time I actually spent with them. Pete, a trumpeter, and Richard, a saxophonist, were in the band and attended all of Jonetta's games.

The four of us were honor students and had been as long as we could remember. We took most of the same classes and found ways to sit near one another in each class. The competition among us was friendly and the banter was comfortable. With them, I felt like I belonged.

CHAPTER SEVENTEEN

"Hey Kathy!" A voice called to me from behind. "Wait up!"

I turned around to see Richard jogging up behind me, sax case in his left hand, bulging backpack slung over his right shoulder. I grinned broadly.

"What's up, Richard," I said when he caught up.

"Band practice cancelled. Thought I'd try to catch up with you."

"Cool. We can walk together."

Bwamp! Bwamp! The car horn startled us and we both jumped back, away from the curb.

"Hey girl!"

The familiarity of the voice jerked me around. Sure enough there was the beat up white Ford pickup easing behind us. Johnny Ray's head stretched toward the lowered passenger side window.

"Hey Johnny Ray," I said nervously. "What are you doing over here this early in the day?"

"What? A man can't come see his woman and children when he pleases?" He stopped the truck, winked at me, and then focused his attention on Richard. "Who's that?" he asked with a jerk of his head, crude smile on his face.

"A friend," I said quickly, glancing at Richard.

"Just a friend huh? Looks more like a boyfriend to me."

Johnny Ray's tone and the set of his mouth made the hairs on my neck stand up. I shifted my weight and glanced away from him back to Richard. His eyes were as big as silver dollars and he moved the sax case from one hand to the other.

"Well, get in," Johnny Ray said, leaning across the seat opening the door.

"I don't mind walking," I said hopefully.

"Now why would you do that – unless you're trying to sneak in some more time with your *boyfriend* here?" He grinned.

"I told you, he's not my boyfriend." I turned to Richard. "I'll see you later, okay?"

He looked from me to Johnny Ray and back to me. "Uh, okay."

I crossed in front of Richard and made my way slowly toward the truck not daring to glance up. Richard stayed rooted to the spot as I slid in, yanked the heavy door shut, and Johnny Ray pulled off.

The radio played a neo soul groove by Anthony Hamilton. It was one of my favorites, but it was all wrong for this ride. I wanted to adjust the dial, but that would be too risky. I didn't want to give Johnny Ray any ideas.

"You can admit it to me, you know," he said looking at the side of my face.

I kept my eyes trained on the car in front of us.

'Come on, you can tell old Johnny Ray. I can keep a secret. And I know you can." He reached over to put his hand on my leg. I carefully pushed it away.

"I don't have anything to tell."

"You're about the right age to have a boyfriend. Your mama's just old fashioned, that's all. But as I man, I understand."

"I told you he's not my boyfriend," I said through gritted teeth.

"Umph."

I breathed a sigh of relief when we finally pulled into our apartment complex. I was out of the car before the wheels stopped rolling. I could feel his eyes on me as I walked up the steps and through the door.

"Mama! I'm home."

"It's about damn time. You've put me behind in getting dinner ready for these kids and now they're all fussy."

She shoved one of the crying babies into my chest. I shifted my books into one arm and took the boy in the other. "Shhh," I whispered close to his face, bouncing him gently.

"Do you want me to go to the store for you today?" I asked.

"No, I've figured something else out now. Just take that screaming boy and find out what his problem is. He may be wet or something. Then get these kids out of here so I can---"

"A man's been out working all day and he don't want to come home to no bitching and griping," Johnny Ray said, catching Mama by surprise.

Mama spun around so fast I thought she might fall. "Johnny Ray!" Her eyes lit up. "Hey baby!" She sashayed over to him, wrapped her arms around his neck and kissed him hard on the mouth. I averted my eyes.

"Daddy! Daddy!" Margaret Ann squealed jumping up and down.

Johnny Ray swatted Mama hard on the butt then strode over to his exuberant daughter, picked her up, tossed her into the air and caught her easily. His muscles bulged through his tight shirt. Margaret Ann giggled with delight and I was mad at myself for being jealous.

I laid my books on the coffee table, and then shifted the baby onto my hip. "Dang!" He'd left a wet imprint on my shirt that smelled strongly of pee and poop. "Ugh!" I snatched him off me and held him an arm's length away. "What's in your diaper," I said frowning, taking him into the bathroom to get the wipes and a diaper.

I laid him on the floor. While he wailed, I removed his heavily soiled, soaking-wet diaper. "Whew! Boy you are really smelly." Holding my breath, I cleaned the poop from his bottom and legs, and then reached around to the stack of off-brand disposable diapers to put on a fresh one. His wailing faded into a whimper. I lifted him and whispered, "I wonder what she's been doing all day." He giggled as if he understood. I put the now smiling boy down with the rest of the toddlers and went to change my shirt.

"Kathy! Didn't I tell you to get these kids out of here?"

"Yeah, girl. You'd better listen to your mama," Johnny Ray scolded, as if he had some authority to tell me anything.

I rolled my eyes at him, and then turned to the kids. "Okay guys, who wants to go outside?"

A chorus of "me" rang out.

"Put your shoes on and line up!"

After what seemed like an eternity of chasing kids around the common courtyard of the apartment complex, we were called inside to eat. Finally with the kids gone, the dishes put away, my homework finished, Margaret Ann and I could get bathed and settled in. But my peace was short lived as Mama burst into our room. Her breathing was labored and her chest heaved up and down. I thought she was having a heart attack.

"Mama, what's wrong," I asked throwing back the covers and jumping out of bed.

"I knew you were lying to me, you ungrateful little bitch!"

"Huh?"

"Now I know what took your ass so long to get home," she spat. "You were out with some boy this afternoon! Sneaking around with your *boyfriend*, trying not to get caught. Well guess what. You was caught!"

"But Mama----"

"Don't you 'but Mama' me. Johnny Ray saw you! He told me everything. You know I don't like liars, Kathy, and that's just what you've become. You're a liar and I'll never believe another word you say."

She sucked in on her cigarette. "I have half a mind to beat you good." Her face was flushed and I knew that if I even looked at her the wrong way she'd get one of Johnny Ray's belts.

"I'm sorry Mama. I didn't---"

"Don't you say another word to me, Kathy. Right now I can't stand the sight of you."

I winced.

"And I sure as hell ain't coming to no year-end program now – essay contest or not. Now go tell that to your little *boyfriend*!"

She stared at me a long time, huffing her breath and taking long drags on the cigarette.

I should have invited Aunt Grace, I thought. Of course, if Mama had come and seen Aunt Grace there, she really would have gone off the deep end. Plus, I might not even win. How embarrassing would that be?

From around the door, Johnny Ray's hand appeared on Mama's shoulder and reached down to the tip of her breast. He leaned around, stroked her hair, and kissed her softly on the cheek; all the while his eyes bore a hole into me. I dared not look away. "Let's go to bed, baby. You can deal with her," he said, flicking a hand in my direction, "in the morning."

CHAPTER EIGHTEEN

The following morning in first period, I tuned out Mr. Davis' boring lecture and poured my soul into my notebook. It was the beginning of my seventh iteration of the same essay. But after yesterday, I saw it all so clearly. By the end of second period, I hadn't heard a word of Spanish, but the first full draft of *The Greatest Challenge of My Life* was finished. When Jonetta, Pete, Richard and I filed into sixth period Honors English, it had been written, edited and rewritten.

Here it goes, I thought, making my way past Heather and Amy to hand my essay to Mrs. Scott.

"You sure cut it close, Kathleen," she said taking my handwritten pages and stapling them together.

I studied the floor.

"Most of the students submitted their essays – typed I might add – earlier in the day. Of course, Heather and Amy both turned theirs in yesterday."

I looked up to catch Mrs. Scott smiling proudly in their direction. I rolled my eyes. What was I thinking? How stupid of me to put my heart out there for the entire world to see. The whole school would find out the truth and I would become the laughing stock. I almost snatched the paper back, but just as my mind told my hand to move,

Mrs. Scott slid the pages into a manila folder labeled,
School-Wide Essay Contest.

"Anything else," she asked.

My face flushed. A few people snickered. "No," I
mumbled, turning, eyes down, quickly finding my seat.

I walked home in a depressed state despite Jonetta's
best efforts to cheer me up. Today I wished that she had
basketball practice. I wanted to be alone. Actually, I
wanted to die.

The rest of the day was no better. Three of the kids
had colds and their noses ran incessantly. Fussy, clingy
and feverish, they needed constant attention. I was so busy
taking care of them I almost forgot to go to the store for
Mama's cigarettes and Cokes.

"Why so sad?" a male voice asked out of no where,
startling me as I lingered on the beverage aisle.

I jerked around and the case of Coca-Cola I was
holding rammed right into his thigh. "Oh! I am so sorry,"
I stammered.

"It's cool," he said dusting the point of impact with
the back of his hand. His piercing blue eyes met mine and I
looked away. He had the lean, muscular physique of a jock
and straight teeth, with moist pink lips like a model. I was
suddenly aware that my naturally curly hair was a frizzy
mess and that I probably had kid mucus somewhere on my
shirt.

"So, why so sad today?" he asked again.

"I'm not sad," I said, shrugging my shoulders and
making a face. "What makes you think I'm sad?"

"Usually when you come in, you're all bouncy."
He bobbled his head from side to side.

"Bouncy?" I mimicked his movement. "What's that
supposed to mean?"

"It means, you have a bouncy sort of walk and your
hair sways when you move."

"It does?"

"Sure. And you usually speak to everyone you pass."

I scrunched my face. "I do?"

"Umm...yeah."

"And...You know this how," I asked moving down the aisle.

He followed. "I watch," he said matter-of-factly. "I'm observant."

"So do you watch all the customers?"

"No!" He feigned offense, "Only the pretty ones."

My face felt hot. In addition to being super cute, he was smooth. Not knowing what to say, I studied the bags of potato chips lining the shelves opposite the carbonated beverages.

He stood beside me for a minute, and then stuck out his hand. "I'm Andy."

I hesitated. "Kathy," I said finally taking his grimy hand. His short nails were dirty, and I discretely wiped my hand on my pant leg.

"So, you must live nearby," he ventured.

"Why would you say that?" I asked, uncomfortable with how much he seemed to know about me.

"Because you're here practically everyday."

Embarrassed, I looked away again. It made sense, but I didn't know anyone actually noticed. I came; I got Mama's stuff; I left. What's to notice? Now, I was wasting time. Mama would be mad if it took me too long. "Yeah... well, I have to go now," I said, abruptly walking away.

"It was nice meeting you," Andy called after me.

"Yeah, you too," I said over my shoulder without pausing.

Walking home I replayed the scene in my head. What an idiot, I thought. Could I have been any ruder? He'll probably never say anything to me again. But why hadn't I noticed him before? And if he had been watching me, why would he pick today to say something? I wondered if he would be at work the next day.

He was. And I was glad that I'd made an effort to look nice. I vowed to do that every time I went to the store from then on. He usually spotted me first and came over to say "hi". If five minutes passed, I found myself looking for him. Andy always complimented something about me. Some of his comments made me blush. Walking to the store quickly became my favorite afternoon pastime.

CHAPTER NINETEEN

As much as I looked forward to walking to the store, I had developed a total disdain for walking to school. In the springtime, the mile and a half between the door of the school and the door to my apartment left a lot of distance for rain storms, sweaty arm pits, and bad hair days. Its only benefit was the time it provided me to think.

Having already turned in my essay, these days I thought mostly about Andy. The way his blue eyes sparkled when he smiled, how easily his laugh seemed to come, the way he tossed his head just so to clear the strands of black hair that fell to his face; all of it captivated my imagination. I closed my eyes and conjured up an image of him walking with me.

Suddenly, my foot caught on the uneven sidewalk, jerking me into the present. Stumbling forward, I stepped in a puddle of water, and nearly sideswiped a tree before finding my footing. At least this time I didn't drop my books. Heart beating wildly, I glanced around to see if anyone had noticed. No one had. I was still pretty much invisible – except to Andy. And that was what I like most about him: he saw me. For the first time in my life someone actually saw *me*.

It was the end of my junior year of high school and as of today, I had done nothing to leave a mark – nothing to be remembered by. As I walked into class, I wondered: if I were to drop off the face of the Earth today, aside from Jonetta, Richard and Pete, who at this school would know I was ever there? The cruel truth: Amy and Heather. Ugh.

"Teachers and students," boomed a voice way too close to the intercom, "please excuse the interruption." There was a brief pause as papers ceased their shuffle and conversations trailed off. "Due to this afternoon's assembly, today's class schedule will be abbreviated as follows..." A raucous cheer broke out in our classroom drowning out the rest of the announcement. Even as the teacher struggled to regain order, she knew it was unnecessary. The abbreviated schedule was nearly as routine as the regular schedule. Each class would be forty minutes long, rather than the usual fifty-five minutes and lunch periods would begin a half hour earlier. The assembly would be held at the end of the day.

Classes flew by. As soon as a teacher introduced the day's material, it was time to pack-up. We loved abbreviated schedules. No one wanted to listen to boring teaches drone on and on about something few of us understood and even fewer cared about. In these classes, those sitting in the back would insert an earbud and listen to iTunes. Others clustered their desks, passing notes and whispering among themselves. Some just napped. The interesting teachers made the most of the abbreviated schedules by nixing the lesson plan in favor of participatory discussions about the topic of the day.

Because some of her students had entered the essay writing contest, the winner of which would be announced in today's assembly, our biology teacher explained the nervous system and how anxiety and excitement affect the body. We discussed adrenalin, fight or flight, and other autonomic nervous system functions. It was good to be able to put names with the feelings I was experiencing. My stomach was in knots. I couldn't concentrate. I fidgeted nonstop. I wanted to win, but I was scared to death of reading my essay to the entire student body.

My heart was pumping hard; my blood was flowing so loudly I could hear it pounding in my ears; my breathing was shallow; and I had so much energy I could have run home and back without a break. I didn't want to talk about the contest or the assembly. I didn't even want to think about it anymore.

But that was not to be the case. Jonetta was constantly in my ear whispering some version of "...and the winner is..."

"Stop it!" I whispered hotly through clenched teeth. "I'm trying to focus."

"No you're not," she whispered back with a laugh. "You just want me to think you are."

When the bell finally rang for us to assemble, I was relieved. The torture was finally coming to an end. Now, if they would just blurt out the winner and let us all go home. Of course, too much had been made of the contest for that to happen. Teachers had devoted class time describing ways to structure the essays. The various grades had been pitted one against the other to find out which could produce a winner.

The seniors were all pumped up. After all, they were the cream of the crop and the AP English students were already celebrating their presumptive victory. Some of us would like nothing better than to knock them off their high horses, but most of the junior class could have cared less. The sophomores were cocky now that they had a freshman class beneath them to kick around. A couple of them even thought they were good enough writers to beat the seniors. We laughed at them. The freshmen were just glad to have been invited to the party.

Nearly one thousand students stood in unison to recite the Pledge of Allegiance as the Color Guard presented Old Glory and the Tennessee state flag. Our ROTC unit was recognized as one of the best in the state for five years running and we gave them a resounding round of applause. The redheaded freshman class president gave the welcome and was heckled by some obnoxious seniors as she left the stage. Mr. Rogers, our principal, stood and looked in their general direction and things settled down. The chorus performed a song from *Dreamgirls*, followed by Mrs. Scott, who gave a description of the essay contest – its topic, the rules and an introduction of the judges. A five-member panel, which included Mrs. Scott; Dr. Hunter, the AP English Professor; one of the guidance counselors; Mr. Rogers; and one student representative, who just happened to be Amy's boyfriend, Kyle.

My head fell forward. So much for that, I thought.

Jonetta rolled her eyes. "Whatever," she whispered too close to my ear. "You still have this. He's just one vote."

"Stop it!" I hissed back. Even if I had written the best essay, there was no way Dr. Hunter would ever let anyone beat out one of his AP students. Kyle's vote would just be another nail in the coffin.

CHAPTER TWENTY

The chorus finished its second song, this time from
A Chorus Line. The main part of the tune is: I hope I get
it…I really hope I get it…" It was both appropriate and
annoying. I rolled my neck from side to side, trying to
work out the tension that had only increased as the day
wore on. Why were they drawing this out? Why couldn't
it be over already?

"And now," said Mrs. Scott, taking the microphone
again, "the time has finally come to announce this year's
first, second and third place winners of the first ever Shelby
High School school-wide essay writing contest: *The
Greatest Challenge of My Life*."

Instantly all noise ceased. I sat stock still. Not even
Jonetta spoke.

"Taking home the enviable third place trophy
is…David Austin!"

A series of shouts and whistles followed a thin,
shaggy-looking boy as he casually made his way from the
top row of the crowded auditorium. Unkempt hair covered
his eyes and his vintage Grateful Dead t-shirt and black
jeans were accented with silver chains that matched the
ones covering the large holes in his ears.

"David's essay, titled…" Mrs. Scott pursed her lips and looked out at the audience from beneath her glasses, "…School Sucks and that's The Greatest Challenge of My Life…"

The auditorium erupted into laughter and cheers. Seconds later, David was at the podium adjusting his hair to see well enough to fully appreciate the moment, before Mr. Rogers regained control. With a last stern glance at the student body, he slowly returned the microphone to Mrs. Scott.

"Despite the title," Mrs. Scott continued, turning to make a face at David, "David's essay is quite good – albeit with a strong sense of humor – for a sophomore who hasn't yet been through the rigors of my class. Next year, he'll know just how much school sucks!"

A second burst of laughter circulated through the assembly and Mr. Rogers jumped to his feet. We calmed ourselves.

Mrs. Scott continued, "Our second place trophy winner in *The Greatest Challenge of My Life* essay writing contest is…Amy Winters!"

Wild applause went through the crowd as our homecoming queen, cheerleading captain, and junior class valedictorian stood and bowed gracefully from the third row, front and center. She raised her right hand and gave us her best beauty queen wave. But her smile was stilted and didn't quite reach her eyes. Even from my seat high above hers, I recognized the look. She's the best at everything. Not even she could mask the disappointment of coming in second. On stage, Amy tucked her perfect blonde hair behind her ear, wetted her perky pink lips, and pasted on the perfect smile.

"Who could have beaten her?" I whispered to Jonetta.

"You."

"Whatever."

"And now," said Mrs. Scott, sounding like a seasoned game show host, "the moment you've all been waiting for! The first place and grand prize winner of *The Greatest Challenge of My Life* essay writing contest is...Kathleen Sumner!"

Jonetta jumped up so fast, I thought she had won. Her scream rose above the cheering and pierced the eardrums. Richard and Pete stumped their feet on the bleachers. Others followed suit. My three best friends started chanting "Kathy! ... Kathy! ... Kathy!" The chant took hold and soon it seemed the entire student body of Shelby High School was saying my name. Unbelievable...they were saying *my* name.

I couldn't move. It was a joke, I told myself. Mrs. Scott would say she was kidding and the real winner would be announced. It just wasn't possible.

"Kathleen Sumner!" Mrs. Scott said again this time leaning into the microphone.

"Kathy!" Jonetta shouted, popping me on the arm. "Get up!"

I stared up at her blankly. She grabbed my arm and pulled me out of my seat. The cheers exploded and my heart jumped into my throat. I was lightheaded, afraid to move. Jonetta turned my body and pushed me toward the aisle. I'm not sure how I made it onto the stage.

Mrs. Scott hugged me. Then David and Amy stiffly did the same. Mr. Rogers handed me a shiny black plaque and an envelope containing the $50 gift card. The others on the stage, including Kyle, shook my hand. Looking out at the sea of faces, tears formed in my eyes. I had won. I had actually won! Fighting hard to stop myself from either laughing or crying, I was stricken with fear. Would I be able to say anything without breaking down? Could I actually read my essay?

Looking out at the sea of faces, my stomach lurched. *Focus*, I told myself. It was time to come clean, to be who I really am. I reached up to adjust the microphone and it fell with an amplified thud, setting off shrieking feedback.

Sweat beads formed on my forehead and upper lip. Mrs. Scott was at my side in a flash reattaching the microphone and placing it at the appropriate height. She cleared her throat to regain the crowd's attention, cut me a look that said, "get it together" and returned to her seat.

"*Facing the Truth: Confessions of a Fatherless Child*," I began softly, my voice quivering as I read the title. "During my life, my father has been everything from a wealthy Frenchman to an American war hero. He's been Chechnyan, and he's been Arabian. He's been alive and he's been dead. But what he hasn't ever been is a real person, at least not to me."

I paused, waiting for the jeers to begin. When they didn't materialize, I took a deep breath and plunged ahead not daring to look up. "The truth of the matter is: beyond conception, my father did not exist and my mother claims no memory of him. No name. No physical description. No family tie. Nothing. No example of unconditional love. No protector. No provider. No hero. No one."

My voice grew stronger with each word. I found a rhythm punctuated by audience reactions. They gasped when I revealed my mom's admission that she didn't know who my father had been and they laughed at my attempts of humor. The more I revealed of myself, the more confident I felt.

By the time I delivered the last paragraph, "The greatest challenge of all of this has been figuring out that being father-*less* does not actually make me anything *less*. No less of a person. No less special. No less worthy. In fact, because of it, I now know that I am a stronger person, more special in my uniqueness, and very much worthy of all that life has to offer." The crowd was on its feet clapping and cheering. Behind me, Mrs. Scott was wiping a tear and our principal was coming towards me, arms outstretched, ready to encircle me in a bear hug.

Making my way down the steps of the stage, I was met by teachers congratulating me on my award and students telling me what a great speech I'd given. One girl said I'd made her cry. Even Peabody, who doesn't talk to anybody, came over to talk to me.

"I liked your speech," he ventured, looking down at his shoes such that I could barely hear him.

"Thank you," I replied ready to brush past him and catch up with my friends. When he didn't move, I assumed that meant he wasn't finished and leaned in closer.

"Listening to you," he continued, "was like hearing my own journal come alive."

"Huh?" I furrowed my brow. What was he talking about?

"What you said up there," he motioned with his head, "that is exactly how I feel."

"What do you mean?"

This time he looked up and our eyes locked. "I mean that I'm like you. I don't have a father either. I guess I haven't handled it as well as you have. But it never occurred to me that there was anybody else in the world who didn't even know who their father was."

I was shocked. Although we'd been in school together since sixth grade, I barely knew Peabody, and never would have guessed we'd have anything in common.

"I've never said that out loud to anyone," he continued shyly. "I just wish in all these years, I could have had your courage. I wish that I had had your strength."

In that moment I understood all that Peabody had had to endure because of his father's abandonment. His mother had taken to drinking. She'd been unable to function, unable to give him any of the comforts of home.

Wow, I thought. Maybe my mom hadn't been quite as terrible as I'd made her out to be. I did have clean clothes. There was food in the house. My level of care was far from perfect, but it wasn't nearly as bad as what Peabody had had to contend with. I wanted to hug him and make his hurt go away the way I'd wished someone would have hugged me so many times before.

"Girl," Jonetta said breathlessly, finally breaking through the throng of people surrounding me and putting an end to the conversation. "You were like a preacher up there! All you needed to do was pass the plate."

"Yeah," Richard chimed in, slapping me on the back. "You had 'em crying in the aisles."

"How did it feel to be up there talking and have the entire student body hanging on your every word?" Jonetta asked anxious for the details.

"Were they?"

"Were they? What?"

"Hanging on my every word."

"What are you talking about? Weren't you there? Of course they were hanging on your every word. What about 'crying in the aisles' didn't you understand?"

"I don't know. It was crazy. It was like I was in a different place from everyone else. I mean I could hear people so clearly. Every sound was amplified in my ears. My senses were heightened as if I had super powers. But my mind was focused and it was like I was alone and talking to myself. And I felt so alive. So..I don't know...strong?" I looked at my friends willing them to understand.

"All I know is: you were great."

"Yeah, really awesome."

I had been talking and smiling for so long my face hurt. As people continued to talk around me, my thoughts drifted. I was actually glad Mama hadn't come. She probably wouldn't have understood what I was trying to say and it would've taken me forever to smooth things over. Humph. But I did miss having Aunt Grace seeing me on stage. If I was as good as my friends said I was, she would have been so proud. I wish I would have invited her. Ooh, and Andy. I couldn't wait to share this day with him. I was suddenly ready to go home. Surely Mama needed something from the store.

"Kathy!" Pete had joined us and I hadn't noticed. I turned. "You were so good up there! Everybody's talking about you."

I couldn't help but laugh. "Well, this is the first time everybody's been talking about me and I was happy about it."

CHAPTER TWENTY-ONE

The excitement around winning the contest was fun; but, unfortunately, short lived. It's most lasting effect would be to give Heather and Amy new ammunition for their verbal attacks. But since I'd beaten them both in the essay writing contest, I had a few bullets of my own I could fire. Still, that would have to wait until next year. For now, everyone was occupied with their plans for summer. During the school year, I had three friends who made me forget my home life for a few hours. Summer vacation was about to bring that to a screeching halt. The end of the school day would usher in the beginning of three months of purgatory – a hell I would have to walk through alone.

All around me people were talking about, and looking forward to, summer break. The very thought of it made my head hurt. I would essentially be locked in an apartment all day with a bunch of other people's kids and no way to escape. And who knew what Johnny Ray would get in his mind to do. But like it or not, I was stuck and there was nothing I could do about it.

"We'll call you," Richard promised

"Next year will be here before you know it," Pete said.

"Hang it there girl. Don't let them get you down," Jonetta whispered, hugging me.

Despite their assurances, when I left school for the last time, I felt completely and utterly alone. Walking home, the gathering storm clouds fit my mood. The only thing that would have made it worse would have been for it to have rained. There was nothing worse than going to the store in the rain and walking home carrying a soaking wet bag of groceries. I hurried home as fast as I could, hugging a year's worth of papers, folders and binders.

Entering the house, I was greeted by the familiar wails of babies, chatter of toddlers, and incessant droning of cartoon characters on television. "Mama! I'm home," I said following the whiffs of smoke into the kitchen.

"Here," she said pushing onto me the toddler she'd had perched on her own hip. The little girl reached out, put her arms around my neck, and held on for dear life, which was good since I hadn't yet freed my arms to grab her.

I found a spot on the cluttered kitchen table to sit everything, and then balanced the girl on one side while I wiggled the other side out of my jacket. Before I could finish, two other kids had wobbled their way over and grabbed onto a leg.

"Kathy! Kathy!" Margaret Ann called running in.

"Hey Mar Mar!" I said smiling. "How's my favorite sister?"

"I'm your only sister, silly."

I tussled her hair. "I knew that."

"Spin me, Kathy! Spin me!"

I put the little girl down and extracted myself from the others. They started to fuss so I promised to spin each of them in turn.

"Move back now," I warned. Placing my hands beneath Margaret Ann's arms, I twirled her high into the air. She giggled and her laughter made me feel better.

"Again," she said wobbling from the dizziness. I spun her several more times until the cries of the others got too loud to ignore. It was their turn. I twirled so many, I became dizzy myself.

"Alright! Enough of that silliness," Mama said. "Stop playing and start changing those kids' diapers and when you're finished, I need you to go to the store to pick up some milk and peanut butter. And bring me a pack of cigarettes and case of Cokes. I ran out today and had to walk to the Laundromat to get some more. Do you have any idea how hard it is to take all these kids all the way over to the Laundromat?"

I almost laughed out loud, but knowing better, I groaned instead, "But Mama, it's starting to rain. Can't Johnny Ray pick that stuff up on his way home tonight?"

"Don't you ask me nothing about Johnny Ray. He's the man of this house and what he picks up and don't pick up ain't none of your business."

"But Mama---"

"Don't you talk back to me. Go on now, you'd better get started before the rain really starts coming down."

"Yes ma'am."

While I was worried that my hair would frizz in the rain, I was really excited about seeing Andy. We had grown to something more than friends and I'd tasted the sweetness of his lips a couple of times now. I liked the warmth of his breath and the firmness of his kiss. I smiled at the memory as I set up a work area on the floor near the window so I could watch the rain. I arranged the diapers and wipes and grabbed the diaper cream and powder. Working from youngest to oldest, I cleaned, dried, and toileted 11 children. Nearly a full house today, I thought, then tried to figure out who was missing.

"Kathy, stop daydreaming and hurry up!"

I sighed heavily. "Okay," I said. But my mind said: there are worse things I could be daydreaming about.

I got up and dug through the closet for an umbrella, found one that was mostly intact, and headed out. My feet were soaked and I thought my shoes might come apart before I made it back, but Andy's shift was ending and, much to my relief, he offered to give me a ride home. He drove a gold Maxima. It had belonged to his mom who gave it to him after he graduated from high school. The leather was as soft as his touch.

He held my hand as he drove, expertly maneuvering through the late afternoon traffic. I settled back into the slightly reclined seat, relaxing for the first time in hours. The windshield wipers kept rhythm with the rain and we rode mostly in silence except for the occasional direction on where to turn. I used the time to check out the car. It seemed unusually clean for a guy's car. The only things I noticed were the black and gold tassel from his high school mortarboard hanging from the rearview mirror, a yellow Wendy's cup in the cup holder, and a single cigarette butt in the ashtray. Still, the car smelled fully of Andy. The masculine scent of cigarette smoke and cologne lingered in the air and between the rain drops, windshield wipers, hand holding, and manly aromas; I was feeling a little light headed. Andy pulled the car over a few yards from the entrance to our section of apartments and leaned in for a kiss.

Soft and gently his tongue explored my mouth and crowded my thoughts. Thoughts that surely said I should leave were swallowed whole by those that told me to stay. And when his hands joined the exploration, I couldn't hold on to any thoughts at all. Even breathing was a challenge as my senses took over and I pressed myself nearer to him, feeling like I might smother under his weight, but willing him closer still.

His mouth found my neck and his fingers intertwined with my curls, guiding my head until I swayed and swooned with the scrolls he drew there and on my shoulders. Every nerve in my body was strained and pulled toward him and there was an unfamiliar pulse deep inside me that beat harder and faster than even my breath was coming.

Somewhere in the midst of all this, I was vaguely aware that my mind was trying to send me a message. I ignored it. I pushed it away, focusing more intently on the sensations being caused by Andy's lips and fingers and thighs. I shut my eyes tightly as the pulse within my core grew stronger and stronger. But my mind was determined to re-engage. Trying again to shut it down, I adjusted my head ever so slightly. And in that tiny movement the dull awareness that I'd been ignoring exploded through the fog and shouted: Mama is waiting.

I pushed Andy away with such force; his head hit the dash board. "What was that for?" My face flushed a deeper red than it had ever been.

"I'm sorry," I said touching his face. "It's just that I have to go. My mom is waiting for me."

I opened the door without another word, picked up the grocery bag from the floor, closed the door with my hip, and ran through the rain toward our apartment.

CHAPTER TWENTY-TWO

Slowing my pace as I arrived at the apartment, I wondered if Mama had noticed my tardiness. I leaned the umbrella against the wall and raised my leg to form a shelf on which I could set the bag while I fished the door keys from my pocket. Fortunately, it was relief rather than anger that registered on Mama's face as I pushed open the door.

"Oh good," she said. "When you put that stuff away, you can pour me a Coke over ice. Then take these kids off my hands for a while. I need a minute." I was okay with that. The truth was, I could use a minute myself. I put the groceries away, handed Mama her Coke on ice and a fresh carton of Filter King Kools, and gathered up the kids. I decided to take them outside to the back porch. It was covered and we both could be out of the rain and away from the glare of Mama's watchful eye.

I took a roll of toilet tissue outside with me to wipe the kids' constantly running noses. Between wipes I led them through multiple rounds of "Ring around the Rosie" and "London Bridge Is Falling Down", rolled the ball with them until I got tired of retrieving it from the rain, and told stories until it was time to go inside to greet their parents.

On Monday morning, my first official day out of school, I woke to screaming in my ear. Mama was attempting to lay one of the babies beside me. "Wha---"

"Be quiet! She's sleepy and I need somewhere to lay her down."

"What's wrong with your bed?"

She cut me a look. "Johnny Ray's in there. It's still raining and since he's working outside right now, he ain't going in today."

I wiped my eyes with the palm of my hand and glanced past the baby's head over at the clock. 6:30, it read. I groaned, then picked her up and laid her on my chest. She wailed louder. I patted her back; still she screamed. I yawned, pulled back the covers and stood with the baby. She calmed down a bit, but was still crying. I started pacing around the room, which seemed to do the trick. After a while, she fell asleep. I laid her gently in my bed and began to walk away. But the minute she could no longer feel my hand on her back, her screaming resumed.

"Shut that baby up," Johnny Ray shouted from the other bedroom.

I stuck out my tongue in his general direction, picked up the baby and started walking again. Just as she drifted off, there was a knock on the front door. I dared not move, fearing that she would awaken. As time passed the knocking grew louder and more incessant. "Kathy," Mama yelled. "Don't you hear that door?"

The baby woke in a fit. "Ugh!" I yelled.

"Just get the damn door!"

Turning the deadbolt, I opened the door to let in the twins. It was a steady stream of kids after that. Some were crying, others were wet, and the baby refused to be put down, even for a second. I managed to pour six bowls of cereal and change two diapers with the baby alternating between my hip, shoulder, and lap. When Mama and Johnny Ray finally emerged from the bedroom, the kids were quietly watching cartoons and the baby was asleep on my lap.

"Since you've got everything under control, I'm going to run some errands with Johnny Ray." They looked at each other and giggled as if sharing a secret.

"But what am I supposed to do with all these kids?"

"Just what you've been doing. I'll be back, Kathy. I ain't going to Timbuktu." She put on a rain coat that hadn't fastened since she'd had Margaret Ann and hurried out the door.

For the next four hours, I chased, cajoled, twirled, fed, diapered and toileted nine children under the age of six. When they finally got back, I was sure Mama would take over and I'd finally be able to brush my teeth, wash my face and get dressed, but that was not the case.

"This place is a mess," Mama announced still standing in the doorway. I looked around. It was a mess. There were crackers smashed into the carpet, toys strewn across the floor, cereal bowls stacked in the kitchen sink, napkins with half-eaten peanut butter and jelly sandwiches littered the surfaces, cookie crumbs were everywhere, and the trashcan was overflowing with dirty diapers and empty juice containers.

"And it stinks in here," Johnny Ray added, joining her in the doorway.

"Well, you're the one who left me here with all these children," I said defensively. "They're your responsibility, not mine!"

In a flash, Mama had taken off her shoe and hurled it at me, barely missing my head.

"Don't you ever tell me what my *responsibility* is. This is my house and if I tell you to do something, then you'll do it – whatever the hell it is. You understand me? Now clean this place up!"

Stung, I wanted to shout back at her, but this was my weekend to visit Aunt Grace and I didn't want to do anything to jeopardize it. I swallowed hard instead, laid the baby on the couch and got up to start cleaning.

My plight was set. Summer wasn't so much a break for me as it was a vacation for Mama. My time was spent taking care of the kids and making treks to the grocery store. At least three days a week I had to go to the store for one thing or another. Fortunately, these were the days that I got to see Andy.

I arranged my shopping trips to coincide with his lunch hour or the end of his shift and he made a point to drive me home each time. Some days we spent those moments alone together exploring one another in ways I didn't know were possible. After these visits I wondered if Mama could tell I was different. I wondered if she knew how much of a woman I was becoming.

But most of the time, we sat in his car and talked. I would share the craziness of my days or the latest shenanigans of Johnny Ray, Mama, Margaret Ann and the kids. He would tell me about the hassles his parents were giving him about not being in college and his need to figure out what he was going to do with his life. While my mom saw no future for me outside of helping her, Andy's parents were both professionals like Aunt Grace. In fact, his father was an attorney. They expected great things from him.

CHAPTER TWENTY-THREE

That might explain why it felt so strange to me when college brochures started showing up at our apartment. At first I noticed the colorful catalogues with smiling co-ed faces staring up at me from the trash can as I cinched the bags for disposal. Mama automatically threw them out. We didn't need them, she must have surmised, thinking that no one in our house was going to college. For reasons I couldn't explain, I started fishing them out of the trash and intercepting them between the postman and the mailbox when I could.

Although I had never discussed it with Mama, the thought of attending college had crossed my mind a few times. Aunt Grace often talked about the importance of getting a college degree, saying it made for a well-rounded person and potentially increased a person's quality of life. I supposed it was college that had made Aunt Grace so different from Mama. The more time I spent with Aunt Grace, the more desperately I wanted to be strong and polished and successful like her, but deep down, in my most secret place, I worried that my life was destined to be just like Mama's: unhappy and poor and filled with drama. The thought of it made me sad. Then I felt guilty for being sad, which depressed me all over again. Still, even in those dark moments, a voice in my head whispered that there was hope for me yet.

Teachers told me that I had potential. I was mostly an A student. Math was my only real challenge; not so much because it was hard, but because it bored me to tears. I was a writer and there were no stories in math. There was nothing interesting, nothing that I could relate to in numbers.

Even with my dislike of math, I'd earned a 24 on the ACT a couple of months ago and my SAT score had been 1650. Apparently, those weren't bad grades as several schools had written letters to me about early acceptance programs. And hadn't I won the school-wide essay writing contest, beating out even the seniors? There was definitely a chance that I could go to college. And if I could go to college, then maybe I really could be like Aunt Grace.

Sometimes, I would daydream about going off to another city to attend college. It would have had to be far enough away that Mama and Johnny Ray couldn't show up unannounced, but close enough that I could get home if I had to, especially if Mar Mar needed me. Vanderbilt University in Nashville fit the bill. I had met their representative at our school's college fair. She'd told me that I might qualify for a scholarship and with the school being in Tennessee I would get in-state tuition, making it even more affordable.

I imagined myself living in a dorm room with posters on the wall, music wafting through open doors up and down the hallway, and friends popping in and out of rooms talking about the latest happenings and sharing class notes. I pictured a space in time when I didn't have to answer Mama's paranoid questions about my comings and goings and when I could even go out on a date. Although Andy and I had done a lot together, we had never been on a real date.

The end of summer melted into my senior year with absolutely no acknowledgment from Mama. In her mind, nothing had changed. I went to school. I came home. I walked to the store. I helped her with the kids. Somewhere in all of that I found time to do homework. And while excitement was all around me at school, all I felt was a nagging sense of lethargy. I had no energy. And I felt sick to my stomach almost all the time. Every morning I struggled to get out of bed and when I did, I felt like I was going to throw up.

My mind seemed to be undergoing some kind of metamorphous. I couldn't keep a thought in my head. Classes seemed interminable. I couldn't focus. The lessons were asinine. My friends annoyed me and I could hardly stand to be in the same room with Mama. The smoke from her cigarettes made my head hurt and the scent of food cooking made me nauseous. All I wanted to eat were French fries with lots of salt and all I wanted to do was sit on the back porch and feel the breeze on my face. I offered to take the kids outside everyday just to get some relief and when I got them outside, I did little more than let them run wild, much like my thoughts – they were running amuck. Some days I didn't even feel like walking to the store, even knowing that it would mean spending time with Andy. What was happening to me?

CHAPTER TWENTY- FOUR

I'd thought I had been doing a good job of keeping my concerns to myself. Mama didn't
seem to notice that anything was different. Why would she? All she ever thought about were Johnny Ray, Margaret Ann and the kids. But Jonetta must have sensed that something was amiss. She had taken to walking to school with me in the mornings. Of course her father had a car and typically drove Jonetta to school each day. He'd offered to take me, too, but Mama had an issue with me riding in cars with men so that never happened.

Mama would have had a total meltdown if she'd had any idea of how often Andy drove me home from the grocery store. On his off days he'd even shown up in my school's parking lot to drive me home from school. Since I normally walked the mile home, the ride gave us an extra 30 minutes alone together. He'd taken full advantage of these times and the minutes had always flown by. Maybe Mama knew what would eventually have happened if I'd started taking rides. I felt a stab of guilt over how deeply involved Andy and I had become. She'd never even met him.

Well, not officially. She'd seen him at the store, of course. He'd sacked her groceries – something he usually didn't do. But the clerks had never said anything; they were happy to have had the help. He'd hum a tune while bagging the food, pretending not to pay attention to us. But the minute Mama would turn her head he'd blow kisses, make faces, or wink at me.

He'd enjoyed watching me blush and the more I'd tried not to give him the satisfaction, the redder my cheeks would grow. I'd be exhausted by the time we'd leave the store. But those visits were the most fun. It was as if we'd had a secret code that was known only to us.

This morning, I was moving particularly slow.

"Come on, girl," Jonetta had said exasperated, trying to get me to pick up my pace. "What's wrong with you these days?"

We had been walking past Bojangles' Famous Chicken & Biscuits and before I could respond, the odor from the frying chicken so early in the morning made my stomach lurch. Suddenly, I lost my orange juice and the remnants of last night's dinner.

"Ew!" Jonetta jumped back. "Kathy, that's gross! Are you okay?"

"I don't know. I just want to lie down," I'd mumbled, willing myself to move forward instead.

"Do you want me to walk you back home?"

"No," I said emphatically. "That's the last place I want to be. I'm so sick of my mom. I can't wait until graduation."

"Just four more months," she'd said with a high five that nearly knocked me over. I was weaker than I'd cared to admit. "Oh, sorry."

The moment passed and we'd spent the rest of the walk planned our future for the one thousandth time. I was hoping for a full scholarship to Vanderbilt University. She was attending Jackson State University. I was going to be a writer with a house on the beach and no children anywhere around. She was going to be a scientist and the kind of mother she remembered her own mother had been. Even with the talking and the slower pace, we'd made it to class before the second bell. As we entered class, I wondered if any of that would actually happen.

* * *

"Miss Sumner, may I see you for a moment?" Mrs. Scott's voice appeared out of nowhere as I walked to my third period class. What did she want with me? I'm in Dr. Hunter's Advanced Placement English class this year and don't take any courses from her. But before I could give her an excuse as to why I couldn't join her, the look in her eyes stopped me flat. This wasn't a casual request and saying no apparently wasn't an option.

"Yes ma'am," I answered instead and followed the click of her black peep toe stilettos down the hallway and into her empty classroom. It must be her planning period, I surmised. She closed the door behind me and I wondered again what this conversation could possibly be about.

Mrs. Scott perched herself on the edge of her desk as she always did before beginning a lecture. She pointed to a chair to the left of her desk, motioning for me to sit down. I sat heavily, relieved to no longer be standing. Why was I so tired?

"Kathy," Mrs. Scott began softly, "is everything okay with you?" Her brow was furrowed and I traced the lines around her eyes for a moment.

"Yes ma'am. I'm okay." But as the words were spoken, I found that I couldn't make eye contact, looking instead at the hands lying limply on my lap.

She pursed her lips and studied me for a minute. I averted my eyes knowing that she was trying to read them. I watched the dust bunnies glide across the floor as the air conditioning clicked off. The room grew eerily quiet and I shifted uncomfortably in the hard yellow chair. Mrs. Scott took in a breath.

"I'm glad to hear that you're okay, Kathy, because Dr. Hunter has expressed some concern."

I hadn't expected that. "Concern?" What would Dr. Hunter have to be concerned about?

"Yes. He says that lately you haven't been performing up to your abilities and with the AP exams being held in less than a month, he's concerned." The AP Exams were rumored to be quite rigorous. Last year no one in his class scored higher than a two on a scale of one to five. It took at least a three to earn college credit for one semester of Freshman English and a four or five to earn the full year's credit.

I felt myself becoming defensive. "What does that mean? What does Dr. Hunter know about me and my abilities?"

"Kathy, you're a great writer. You paint beautiful pictures with your words. You capture emotions with your pen that make people see and experience things from a lens only you have discovered. It's a gift, really." She looked away. "I saw it last year – especially in your year-end essay – and Dr. Hunter saw glimpses of it last semester. But this semester, in the last month or so, he said your writing has become perfunctory at best and that you haven't even turned in a couple of assignments. That's just not like you."

"Humph," I said folding my arms across my chest. He'd already given me my first C ever. Wasn't that enough? Why did he have to talk with other teachers about me? When I looked up, Mrs. Scott was searching for answers in my face. I had to give her something. "I've had a lot going on at home," I muttered.

Mrs. Scott leaned closer to my chair. "Kathy, you've always had a lot going on at home. Your teachers have not been oblivious to that. But you've managed to handle the situation at home *and* be an outstanding student here at school. This behavior is something new." She reached for my hands and I reluctantly gave them to her to hold. "Tell me what's really going on."

CHAPTER TWENTY- FIVE

How could I tell Mrs. Scott what was going on with me when I didn't know myself? I didn't know what to say. The room had become unbearably warm and as I stared at our conjoined hands, I realized that I desperately needed fresh air. "I'm fine," I said firmly, retracting my hands and standing up.

But I must have moved too quickly. I was suddenly dizzy and nearly fell over. I sat back down and this time put my head between my knees. When Mrs. Scott spoke again her voice had an edge to it.

"You most certainly are not fine," she said sternly.

"I am," I insisted. "I just got dizzy, that's all."

"No, that's not all." She took my hands. "You're as white as a ghost. Should I call your mother to come get you?"

"No. I don't need to go home. And she doesn't have a car to come get me anyway."

"Kathy, what is going on with you?" Her concern was so genuine, I couldn't help but tell her how I'd been feeling and about the episode on the way to school that morning. She listened and nodded, then leaned in close and asked softly, "Sweetheart, could you be gravid?"

I frowned. Gravid? The word was familiar, but I couldn't quite place it. It had to have been one of our advanced vocabulary words from last year. Mrs. Scott often used them in casual conversation to make us think. Gravid...Oh!

"Pregnant?" I asked indignantly. "Of course not! Why would you even ask me that?" The room started to spin and I leaned back in the chair, legs stretched awkwardly in front of me.

"Well," she said taking my hands in hers. "You just described all the classic symptoms."

"I did not. Did I?" I shook my head. "Did I, really?"

She nodded slowly. As this new information sank in, I was hardly aware that Mrs. Scott was even in the room and not at all cognizant of how intently she was watching me. Andy and I had been together, but only a couple of times in his car, three, if you count the time I had kept my panties on. Surely that wasn't enough to make me pregnant.

Mrs. Scott broke into my thoughts and handed me a cup of lukewarm water. My hands shook as I lifted the Styrofoam cup to my lips.

"How are you feeling now?" she asked as I sipped.

"I'm fine. Probably just coming down with something." Feeling a little steadier, I got to my feet. "I need to get to class," I said more confidently than I felt. Mrs. Scott did not respond right away. But as I turned the doorknob she said, "I'm here, Kathy, if you need anything – even if it's just to talk."

The day swirled around me and I moved through it in slow motion. So lost in my thoughts, I almost didn't notice the gold Maxima parallel parked at the end of the drive.

"What's up, beautiful," Came the familiar voice and I smiled in spite of the day. I loved the way Andy made me feel – pretty, appreciated, special. I walked around to the passenger side and slid into the now familiar car. Still smiling, I accepted his warm, moist kiss, relieved to be in the quiet comfort of his presence.

He held my hand as he drove, telling me about his day at the store. I let the sound of his voice wash over me and exhaled for the first time since being in Mrs. Scott's room. I wondered if I should mention the conversation to him, but immediately decided against it. Not only could I not form my mouth to say the words, doing so would ruin everything – the easy way we talked, the carefree way he moved through life, the way he looked at me as if I were the most precious thing in his world. I shook my head and let the moment pass.

When we reached the drive to the apartment complex and he put the car in park, I laid my head on his chest and let him hold me for as long as I could. The steady beat of his heart, the warmth of his hands, and the scent of his skin calmed my racing thoughts and provided a sense of peace that I held onto with every fiber of my being.

At home, I hardly spoke to anyone as I made my way to my room. To my amazement, Mama didn't call my name for a full half hour. I know because it was three o'clock when I lay down and 3:30 when I opened my eyes again. I'd dreamed about being at a carnival surrounded by colorful, round balloons. I chased after them, but each time I got close to catching one, it would float away. Finally, just as one was within my grasp, Mama shouted my name. I awoke breathing hard and feeling tired.

That night after the kids were gone and Margaret Ann was in her own world of sweet dreams, I lie awake staring at the ceiling. A full blown storm of thoughts was raging through my head. What if I really was pregnant? What would that feel like? I touched my stomach. It felt the same. Or did it? Was it rounder? Firmer? Was there a baby growing inside me? Was I going to be a mother?

Wait. Could a mother go to high school? Would I have to drop out? Could I go to college? I really wanted to go to college. If I didn't go to college, would I have to stay here – in Mama's house? Oh, just the thought of it sent me into a panic. How could we live here, with all those children coming and going? My baby would get lost in the shuffle. There would be no one to take care of her. She'd be hungry and wet until I came home from work to get her. And what kind of work could I possibly do without a college degree? Without a high school diploma?

And what about Andy? His parents had made it clear that they wanted him to go to college. In fact, he was already saying little things that let me know he wouldn't be able to put it off for much longer. And while I'd never met his parents, he certainly wasn't going to take me to meet them pregnant. And if he won't even take me to meet his parents, he definitely wasn't going to marry me. My eyes grew wide with the realization that I would be bringing another fatherless child into the world. Oh God, what have I done? What am I going to do? I held my head to stop the spinning.

As the night grew old and my eyes grew heavy, I drifted in and out of sleep. When I did sleep, it was a fitful rest, filled with uncomfortable dreams I couldn't remember the next morning. These thoughts, and Mrs. Scott's words, replayed themselves in my mind as I walked to school in a haze. By the end of second period, I couldn't take not knowing a single second more. I grabbed my backpack, slipped out the side door beneath the stairwell that led to the alley behind the school, and walked two blocks to the bus stop.

I slid two single dollar bills – my lunch money – into the electronic meter and took a seat by the window.

As the buildings and cars whizzed by, I folded and unfolded my arms, crossed and uncrossed by legs, put the backpack on my lap, then on the floor, then on my lap again. If the bus didn't arrive soon, I might jump out of the window. Twenty minutes later, I was at Planned Parenthood.

CHAPTER TWENTY-SIX

Planned Parenthood was located in a short, squat, tan colored building along a nondescript stretch of busy Poplar Avenue. Tucked between a Sonic Drive-In and a dry cleaner, the building was identifiable only because of the picketers outside holding posters that read, "Babies are being murdered here," or banners that showed unborn fetuses being mutilated. There were six or seven of them shouting at me about how God condemns abortion as I walked toward the entrance. If this was how Christian behaved, it was no wonder Mama didn't take us to church.

The instant the door closed behind me, the noise ceased and I let out the breath I hadn't known I'd been holding. I signed in at the front desk and sat down in a hard orange plastic chair. The chairs reminded me of the yellow one I'd sat in the day before in Mrs. Scott's classroom and my palms began to sweat. Two other girls were in the waiting room, but I didn't make eye contact with either of them. Instead, I hugged my backpack and stared at the floor. What was I doing here? What if someone found out? What if they've noticed that I'm not at school? Would they call Mama? Would Mrs. Scott tell them about her suspicions? Would she guess that I was here and have the truant officer come for me? Would I be arrested?

"Kathleen Sumner." Startled, I jerked my head up. I signaled to the tall blonde lady in blue scrubs, holding a clipboard, got quickly to my feet, flung my backpack over my shoulder, and followed her through a door.

In exam room one, she took my temperature – 98.7, measured my blood pressure – 110 over 83, had me stand on a scale – 119 pounds, and then lean against a measuring stick on the wall – 5 feet, 3 inches. With the physical descriptors recorded, she asked me the questions listed on her clipboard: ever been diagnosed with diabetes? HIV? Heart problems? Headaches? Mental problems? The list went on.

"No," I responded to them all.

"Are you sexually active?"

I hesitated. "Yes."

"Are you pregnant or have you ever been pregnant?" she asked, continuing down the list attached to the clipboard without looking up.

"No, I've never been pregnant." I paused and looked at my hands. "But I might be now." This I said almost in a whisper, afraid if I said it out loud it might actually be true. I was very close to tears and feared that I would breakdown any minute.

It took a second for my words to register with the nurse, because she kept writing, then stopped in mid-stroke and looked up.

"Why do you think you're pregnant?"

"I've been feeling sick and especially tired lately. Yesterday, I threw up for no reason, and later, when I tried to stand up I got really dizzy. The person with me when I got dizzy said that I might be pregnant. I didn't know what else to do, so I came here."

"It's okay. This is a good first step. Have you missed any periods?"

I thought about that. When was my last period? Was I supposed to keep up with this? I searched my mind. "I don't think so. Maybe. I don't know."

"Have you taken a home pregnancy test?"

God, no, I wanted to say. If Mama found a pregnancy test in her house, she'd kill me. She was going to kill me anyway if she ever found out that I'd been to Planned Parenthood. But, the nurse didn't need to know how unstable my family life was, so I simply shook my head and said, "No."

"Okay then, let's get a urine sample." She stood up, crossed the room, reached into a cabinet above the sink and took out a small, clear plastic cup with a lid. She handed the cup to me. "Secure the lid and place the cup in the depository when you're finished. Then come back here, undress and put on this gown. She held it up to make sure I saw it, and then placed it on the end of the examination table. Make sure it opens in the front. The doctor will be in shortly."

With shaking hands, I took the cup, walked the short distance down the hall past pictures of clear-faced smiling peers, happy couples, and pretty, plump babies to the restroom. The pictures painted a very different impression of what Planned Parenthood does from those of the picketers outside. I finished, placed the half-full cup in the depository, which looked more like a wooded medicine cabinet, then returned to the cold exam room, where I took off my clothes, put on the paper gown and sat on the table where the gown had just been.

It wasn't long before the nurse returned with the doctor, who was actually a nurse practitioner.

"Well, your urine gives us a pretty clear indication of pregnancy," said the doctor matter-of-factly. "Still, just to make sure, we'll do a physical examination." The nurse laid several metal instruments on top of a metal tray that she'd covered with a small blue absorbent mat. The doctor pulled a pair of stirrups from the bottom of the examination table. "Put your feet in here and relax your legs."

Yeah right, I thought, as if I could actually relax anything with her watching and you probing and me being exposed. In that moment, a single tear escaped. I closed my eyes and tried to do as I was told, flinching with every touch of her cold gloved hand. Although she described everything she was going to do before she did it, it didn't make it any easier. I'd never had a pelvic exam and I didn't like it.

"Yep, you're definitely pregnant," she announced, with a nod of her head. "About ten weeks."

The lump in my throat rose so quickly, I almost choked. Tears came before words. Even though I hadn't let myself think it, something in me already knew. I closed my eyes again and took a deep breath. "Can I have an abortion, please?" The words were in the form of a plea and were out before I knew it. My hands flew to my mouth as if trying to stuff them back in. But it was too late.

"An abortion? That's a pretty drastic step, don't you think?"

I was as surprised as she was. "Being pregnant is drastic," I said, barely able to speak through the dry lump in my throat.

"Ms. Sumner, it's normal to be a little unnerved by news like this. But there are many options available to you. An abortion should be a last resort." She smiled kindly. "You might find that having a child isn't as bad as you think. Many women have a child at a young age and still go on to do great things."

I simply nodded, my eyes focused on the freckle on the back of my left hand. My mind argued that there was no way to go on to do great things if you couldn't even finish high school, let alone go to college.

"There's also adoption," she continued brightly. "A lot of people can't have children of their own and would love to provide a good home to an infant."

That was easy for her to say, but how would I ever be able to turn my baby over to strangers and expect them to love her and take care of her the way I would? And how could I know that somewhere in the world I had a child and not do everything I could to get to her, to hold her and to make her feel loved? How could I have a child out there and not know for sure that she was alright? What kind of mother would I be? Would kind of person would that make me?

I swallowed hard to force the lump away and to find my voice. "No, I can't have a baby. It would be wrong for me to bring a child into the world that wasn't truly wanted. All my life I've been that child – the accident, the third wheel, the one who didn't belong. How could I saddle a baby with that kind of baggage for the rest of their life? I can't do that to a child. I won't. It wouldn't be fair."

That time she nodded. "I understand," she said softly. "Still, why don't you take a little time to adjust to the news and think about it before you make a decision?"

"I've already made a decision," I said firmly. "I want to have an abortion."

"I respect that," she replied. "However, it's not a procedure that we can do today." My heart fell. I needed to not be pregnant. The longer I stayed that way, the more likely it was that someone would find out. And then where would I be? "There's a mandatory wait in cases like this," she continued. "And before all of that, you'll need to talk with one of our counselors."

I hadn't expected this and was close to panic. "Well, when can we do it then?"

"The earliest we could schedule something would be two weeks from today."

"That won't be too late, will it?" I asked, searching her eyes.

"No, Ms. Sumner, that won't be too late." The doctor removed her gloves and tossed them in the trash, then patted me on the knee. "Take your time getting dressed. The counselor will be in shortly to talk with you." As the doctor turned to leave, the nurse began transferring the instruments from the tray to a plastic bin. I smiled weakly in her direction and waited for her to leave before I stood.

Disappointed, I got dressed in a fog. An overwhelming sadness had taken over and as I listened to the counselor repeat the same options the doctor had already given me, I found it difficult to pay attention. What am I going to do? How could I have let this happen? I was supposed to be smarter than this. I guessed I was really no different from my mother after all. Caught up in the excitement of the moment, I'd forgotten what I'd really wanted out of life. So caught up in giving Andy what he wanted so that he'd like me and stay with me, I forgot to protect myself and stay true to me.

When the counselor finished her talk, she walked me out to the lobby and said goodbye. Once the door closed behind her, I circled around to the front desk and made an appointment for exactly fourteen days later.

CHAPTER TWENTY-SEVEN

Walking back through the picketers, I grew angry.
What did they know about my situation? Who were they to
sit in judgment about the choices I was having to make?
And isn't God supposed to be forgiving? Doesn't He know
all things? Then, He must know what would happen to me
if I had this baby. He must know what would happen to the
baby. Satisfied, I used the last of my energy to push
through their barricade and found myself standing in front
of Sonic. My nose and my stomach had an impromptu
conversation and I realized how hungry I was. Digging
through my backpack, I managed to find enough change to
buy a small order of French fries and was emptying a
packet of salt on them when the bus hissed to a stop.

I climbed on, inserted the last two bills I had, and
not knowing where else to go, I headed back to school
before the final bell. I avoided everyone I knew, sure that
if they looked in my eyes they'd know everything. At
dismissal, Andy was parked in his usual spot and after a
slight hesitation, I opened the door and climbed in.

"Hey," he said leaning toward me for a kiss. I
touched his soft pink lips and quickly turned my head.
"What's wrong, baby?" He took my hand in his and my
heart melted. Every emotion I'd been holding in slid
forward and tears formed behind my eyes.

"Babe," he whispered, genuine concern etched into his face. "Talk to me."

"I'm okay," I said trying to pull myself together.

He brushed a tear from my cheek with his finger and I quivered under its tenderness. "I've never seen you cry before. Tell me what's wrong."

I looked up and into his beautiful blue eyes. How was I going to tell him this awful news? I sighed heavily. "Can we go somewhere to talk?"

"Sure," he said, still looking worried, then pulled out of the parking spot and eased into traffic. Rather than the familiar drive to my apartment complex, Andy drove instead to City Park, where the canopy of hundred year old oaks shaded the renovated play area. He led me through the sprawling climbing structure, past the merry-go-round, over to the deserted swing set, plopped down onto a seat, and motioned for me to sit beside him. It was sweet and the closest we'd ever come to being on a date. I wished we were there under different circumstances.

I settled onto the seat next to his and allowed my feet to play in the dry mulch underneath before either of us spoke.

"What's the matter, baby?" he asked, looking up at me, with concern.

I found the familiar freckle on the back of my hand and took a deep breath. "I went to Planned Parenthood today."

"Planned Parenthood?" Recognition came slowly. "Oh… did you get on the pill," he asked trying to fit things together.

"Not exactly," I answered, fingering the links in the swing's chain.

"What do you mean?"

"Andy," I began, finally looking up. "I'm pregnant."

"Pregnant," he repeated, trying to understand what I'd said. "Pregnant?" He shot up as if his seat had been suddenly set afire. "Damn!" His six foot frame seemed to tower over me, but I didn't have the energy to stand up. I had said it out loud for the first time and doing so had completely drained me.

"Damn," he said again, easing back down onto the swing, looking at his hands instead of me. "My parents are going to kill me. My mother is going to be heartbroken. And my dad – damn – he's going to be furious." He looked away, staring off into the distance of trees and leaves. "Kathy, I am so sorry."

"I know. I'm sorry too." I watched one squirrel chase another up a nearby tree until they disappeared in the branches that seemed to reach into the afternoon sky.

He finally looked at me. His face was contorted, as if in pain. It portrayed the same fear that I had but was too dazed to show. "What are you going to do?"

I pursed my lips. He'd said, what am *'I'* going to do, not what are *'we'* going to do. The words stung. I hadn't gotten pregnant by myself, but apparently I was going to have to handle it by myself. "Have an abortion," I answered flatly.

"Whew…Okay…That's good."

His obvious relief made me angry. Having an abortion was a big deal. I was going to kill my baby. I was no better than a murderer. Hot tears were forming and breathing was getting harder by the second. I wanted to scream, but refused to lose my composure. He was freaking out enough for both of us. I was determined to keep my face expressionless.

"I'm ready to go home now," I said jumping off the swing.

"Now? But don't you want to talk about it?"

"We just did. There's nothing else to say." We were quiet walking back to the car and I noticed that he didn't reach for my hand. Things had changed.

Halfway to my apartment he asked, "So, when are you going to do it?"

I knew exactly what he was asking. "In a couple of weeks. There's a waiting period," I said.

"Oh." More silence. "Does your mom know?"

"No. Right now, you're the only one who knows."

"Are you going to tell her?"

"Probably."

"Damn."

"Yeah, I know."

CHAPTER TWENTY-EIGHT

The rest of the week I walked around just as I had the day before – slowly, avoiding people, especially those who knew me best: Jonetta, Pete and Richard. Jonetta and I hardly talked on the way to school, and I could see that she was beginning to worry. I just couldn't bring myself to tell her. I hadn't even told her that Andy and I had gone all the way. It was a secret I'd been holding onto just for me. Now I felt guilty. How was I going to tell my best friend that not only had I done *it*, I'd also gotten pregnant?

The only person, aside from Andy, I'd told was Mrs. Scott. She'd cornered me again, this time in the cafeteria. She'd been aware of my absence that day – another message delivered by Dr. Hunter – and had noticed how withdrawn from my friends I'd grown. The lady was sharp; I had to give her that. Nothing got past her.

"Kathy, you have to tell your mom," she'd counseled me. "Anything could happen at the doctor's office next week, and she needs to know what you're doing."

"I know; it's just going to be so hard." I'd sighed heavily. She'd patted my hand supportively. But she was right. I had put off the conversation long enough. It was time to break the news.

I waited until all the children had been picked up and I'd completed the tasks Mama had asked me to do before approaching her. As the evening turned into night, I'd worried that Johnny Ray might come home before I'd have the chance to talk to her.

Fortunately, he didn't. When I finally finished, I found Mama sitting up in bed, on top of the covers, in her night gown, with Margaret Ann asleep beside her. It was almost nine-thirty, and the blue glow of the TV was the only light in the room.

"Mama," I said, quietly entering the room, pulling my robe tighter around me as if it would hold me together and shield me from the gathering storm.

"Yeah?"

"Can I talk to you for a minute?"

"Uh huh." Her eyes didn't leave the television screen.

"Um…Mama," I started, still standing in the doorway. "I'm gravid."

"What? You're gravity?" She turned her head and scowled at me. "What the hell are you talking about?" She was annoyed that I was interrupting one of her shows to talk about what must have sounded like gibberish. I'd known she wouldn't understand, but I didn't know how to just come right out and say it. I needed to warm up to the news.

I took a breath and leaned against the wall to steady myself and started again. "I'm pregnant."

She pursed her lips and was quiet for a minute. Then she exploded. "I knew something was wrong with you, the way you've been acting: going around talking about not being able to eat and feeling sick all the time. It's that boy Johnny Ray saw you with, ain't it? I knew you and that boy was screwing."

I flinched. Why did she have to be so crude? She had everything all wrong and made it sound so dirty and gross. I was going to be sick.

"Okay, Mama," I said trying to force my stomach to settle. "I just wanted you to know." I pushed myself off the wall and had half turned to walk out of the door when she started talking again.

"I guess you're going to quit school now."

I spun around. "No," I said shocked by the very idea of it. "Why would you think that? I'm not quitting school."

"And how do you plan to take care of a baby and go to school?"

"I don't. I'm not having it."

"What do you mean, you ain't having it?"

"I'm not having it." I folded my arms defiantly. "I'm going to have an abortion."

"Oh no, you're not," she said matter-of-factly. "This is what you're gonna do. You're gonna go down to the Department of Human Services. I'll go with you. When they ask, you'll tell them you don't know who the baby's daddy is. You can tell them you were drugged or something. That way that boy won't be all up in your business. They'll put you on Aid for Families with Dependent Children and give you Food Stamps. That won't be enough to actually live on, but it will give you some money.

You and the baby can live with me. We'll get a three bedroom apartment when this lease is up so you and the baby can have your own room. You can give me half your welfare check for your part of the rent and use your food stamps to help buy the groceries. With you helping out, I can stop keeping so many of those kids. It'll be tight, but together we can make it. We'll be alright."

I stood in my mother's bedroom and listened to her plan a life for me that was just like hers. The ironic thing was that she was actually trying to be helpful – supportive even. The hopelessness of it brought tears to my eyes. There was no way I was going to do that to myself or my baby.

"No, Mama," I said quietly through the tears, "I'm not going to do any of that. I'm going to have an abortion."

"I told you, you ain't having no abortion. I ain't giving my permission for that. And you can't do it without me."

"Yes, Mama, I can," I said softly, not wanting to argue. The decision was hard enough to come to terms with without having to fight with her about it.

"What did you say to me?" Mama didn't stand for back talk and I usually didn't give it. But this was different. I wouldn't be stuck in a world like hers for the rest of my life, no matter what she said. This time it wasn't just about me; it was about my baby.

"Mama, I'm 17-years-old. I don't need your permission. I didn't even have to tell you."

"Like hell you didn't! Let me tell you something Kathleen Sumner, I am your mother. You will do what I say, when I say it. I brought you into this world and I will take you out. Do you understand me?"

"Yes, ma'am." I sighed. There was no point in arguing with her. Besides, I was mentally exhausted and wanted nothing more than to go to bed. I started to walk out.

"We ain't finished with this conversation, Kathy," she called after me.

CHAPTER TWENTY-NINE

Sure enough, we weren't. Before school the next morning she started in again.

"What are you getting dressed for?" Mama taunted. "School ain't for pregnant girls." I ignored the comment that morning and those that followed over the next several days. But the comments from Johnny Ray were harder to take.

"Heard you went and got yourself knocked up," he said without preamble, leaning himself on the doorframe of my bedroom. The close proximity of his voice caught me by surprise and I looked up startled, regretting it immediately as the crooked smirk on his face made my skin crawl. Mama was in the shower and Margaret Ann was asleep in her bed.

"You should have come to me first," he said grinning. "I'd have shown you how to do it without getting pregnant." Johnny Ray's eyes lingered on me and I turned my back to him busying myself making the bed, uncomfortable beneath his leering gaze.

"Daddy! Daddy!" Margaret Ann called bounding into his arms, breaking the tension. "Watch cartoons with me!"

He smiled at her. "Sure, Baby Girl," he answered looking back at me. "That's probably better than having you being in here with Kathy anyway." She nuzzled against his neck.

What's that supposed to mean, I wanted to ask, but didn't, preferring the separation instead. I exhaled and sat heavily on the bed, watching the two of them walk away and wondering again what it would be like to have my own dad around.

For her part, Mama's taunts were also growing more intense. "You know what I'm going to do?" she asked with two mornings left to go. "I'm going to call your precious *Aunt Grace*," she drew out the name mockingly, "and tell her you're pregnant. Let's see what that does to your little plans."

Her words knocked the wind out of me and a groan escaped before I could hide their impact.

She smiled broadly, obviously pleased with herself. "Ha! I should have thought of that sooner. What will your church-going holier-than-thou aunt think about her sweet little niece having an abortion? You wouldn't want that secret to get out, now would you?"

My heart fell. Mama had figured out the one thing that mattered to me most: disappointing Aunt Grace. The thought had kept me up many nights this last month. I'd hoped to take care of my situation without her ever knowing. Since she and Mama never spoke, I thought I could do it. But that wasn't going to happen now. Mama was too smug. Damn. Hmm. Hadn't that been Andy's reaction when I'd told him about being pregnant? Damn. Suddenly I understood the weight of the word. I wanted to scream it at the top of my lungs. I wanted to say it right to Mama's face, "Damn." But I didn't. I wouldn't. There were lines I just couldn't cross, no matter how badly I wanted to.

"If you want Aunt Grace to know so badly," I answered hotly, "I'll call her myself!" I was furious with Mama for making me tell Aunt Grace, for ruining the one positive relationship I had in my life. But deep down, I was angrier with myself for having gotten pregnant in the first place. It wasn't really about Mama. This was about me.

The following morning I waited until church was over before dialing Aunt Grace's number.

"Kathy," she answered with a smile in her voice. My name must have appeared on her caller ID. "What a pleasant surprise."

"Hey, Auntie." I said trying to sound cheerful, but the affect was whinier than I'd intended.

"What's wrong, sweetie?" Her voice turned serious. "Has something happened?"

"No…Not really…Well…Kind of," I stammered.

I'd decided to place the call in the living room in full view of Mama so that she would know that I'd done it and could hear the conversation first hand, eliminating any need to recount it to her later. I eyed her nervously. She was grinning, clearly enjoying my discomfort. Determined not to breakdown, I adjusted my self, sitting up straighter in the chair. I could do this, I told myself. Taking a deep breath, I plunged ahead.

"Aunt Grace," I said, "I'm pregnant." The moment the words were out, my shoulders collapsed beneath the weight of them and my neck could no longer support my head.

"What do you think of your innocent little niece now?" Mama shouted from the couch.

"Oh, Kathy," Aunt Grace said sighing into the telephone. In the silence I could feel her disappointment. It sat on top of my embarrassment like the heavy layered cake I'd baked for Margaret Ann's birthday. And I had yet to tell her the worst of it.

"I'm sorry," I said sadly.

"Oh sweetie, I'm sorry for you. I'm sorry you're having to go through this."

"Tell her the rest," Mama demanded, interjecting herself into the conversation again.

"Did you have to call me with your mother in the room?" Aunt Grace asked exasperated, her voice revealing mounting frustration. Mama could do that to a person.

"I wanted to," I answered. "She was going to call you if I didn't, and I wanted you to hear it from me."

"That's a lie!" Mama shouted. "She wasn't going to tell you at all. And she still hasn't told you all of it!"

"Agghh!" I was going to loose it.

"Kathy!" Aunt Grace said sharply. "Control yourself." She paused and I breathed deeply, calming myself. "Don't let Sophia get the best of you. Just talk to me as if it were only the two of us."

"Okay."

"Now, are you alright?"

"I will be," I answered believing that to be true. "After tomorrow, I will be."

"What happens tomorrow?"

"I'm going back to the clinic. I've scheduled an abortion."

Aunt Grace gasped. Mama let out a satisfied yelp. And I held my breath. Aunt Grace composed herself quickly. "Have you thought this through, Kathy?" she asked softly.

"Yes. It's what's best."

"Best for whom?"

"For the baby, Aunt Grace," I said pleadingly, willing her to understand. "For the baby." Why didn't people understand that?

"But, there are alternatives, Kathy. There's adoption."

"I know, but that's not a viable option for me, for my situation."

"But abortion...that's so—"

"I know...morally wrong," I finished for her.

"I was going to say permanent. Once you do it, there's no going back; there's no changing your mind. But...since you brought it up...have you talked to God about your choice?"

"Yes," I said tentatively. "I've been praying and in my heart I believe this is the right decision for me. But, you know, God hasn't just come right out and told me what I should do."

"That's the way it works, sweetie. He doesn't usually speak the way we're accustomed to having conversations. He guides us through examples in the Bible and in our everyday lives. He gives us free will – the ability to use our judgment to make decisions based on our relationship with Him and our faith in Him."

"But what if we make a mistake in using our judgment?"

"A mistake, no matter how big or small, doesn't doom us. In fact, the opposite is true. The God we serve is a forgiving and compassionate God. Most of the people written about in the Bible had made mistakes – big ones – and went on to be blessed by God to do great things."

I closed my eyes taking this in.

"My minister sometimes closes his sermons reminding the congregation that Jacob was a cheater. Peter had a temper. David had an affair. Noah got drunk. Jonah ran from God. Paul was a murderer. Gideon was insecure. Miriam was a gossiper. Martha was a worrier. Thomas was a doubter. Sarah was impatient. Elijah was depressed. Moses stuttered. Zaccheus was short. Abraham was old. And Lazarus was dead. But God did miraculous things in their lives. We do not have to be perfect to please God. We just have to be the best we can be and be open to His instruction."

"But the Ten Commandments say: Thou shall not kill."

"Yes, but Jesus said: Love thy neighbor as thy self. And if you love this baby as much as you love yourself and honestly do what is best for the baby, then that is what God requires."

Halfway through Aunt Grace's explanation, Mama got mad and left the room. I don't know what she'd expected; but, whatever it was, she obviously didn't get it. I didn't care. I was numb. I just wanted the day to end and for tomorrow to come.

here.

CHAPTER THIRTY

The procedure was scheduled for ten-thirty on Monday, February 9th , what would be one of the worst days of my life. I woke up nauseous and threw up twice before leaving the house.

"Kathy, where are you going?" Mama asked, seeming to be genuinely concerned. "You're sick, baby. You need to stay home today and rest."

"I'm fine," I replied weakly. "I'm going to school."

"Kathy, this doesn't make any sense. You're trying to act like you're not pregnant, but you are and your body needs rest."

"I'll rest tomorrow," I said, then mumbled under my breath, "It'll all be over then." What did I do that for? Of course she would hear me.

"What do you mean: it'll all be over then?"

"Nothing, Mama. I meant the nausea would be over."

"Kathy, don't you go down to that place today. Do you hear me? I mean it."

"I know, Mama. I'm going to school," I said, pushing past her and walking out of the door. I was late, a blessing in disguise because Jonetta had gone on to school without me, and I wanted to be alone anyway. I'm not sure I said another word that morning. I just moved through the first two classes watching the minute hand take its sweet time navigating the big round circumference of the clock face. The bell rang at 9:55 signifying the end of second period and the beginning of my journey.

I snuck out the side door and on the short walk to the bus stop, I was more keenly aware than ever that a baby was growing inside me. Instinctively, I put my hand on my stomach. What had I done? What was I doing? "Jesus," I said out loud, wishing that He would say something back. But that didn't happen. Instead a thought popped into my mind: I would be a good mother. I would be different from Mama. I would cherish my child. I would protect her and love her and make her feel like she was special, like she mattered. I smiled at the thought.

But, beyond that, I would have nothing to offer her. I'd be a high school dropout, living with my mother, on welfare, and raising yet another fatherless child. What kind of life would that be? I couldn't do that to a child. Alone at the bus stop, I allowed myself to feel the full weight of the decision I'd made, the utter aloneness, the gut wrenching sadness, and I cried uncontrolled, heartbroken tears.

The bus stopped in front of Sonic Drive-In. I turned left, took a deep breath and pushed through the picketers. The clock above the receptionist's desk showed ten twenty-eight.

"It'll be $125," the pretty Hispanic receptionist said.

I nodded and gave her the money Andy had given me the day before. She wrote out a receipt that I stuffed into my purse as I walked to the same hard orange plastic chair I'd sat in two weeks earlier. The girl across from me flipped through an old issue of Good Housekeeping and I stared at the floor.

"Kathleen Sumner," called the receptionist. I returned to the desk.

"Yes?"

"Ms. Sumner, we have a problem," she whispered.

"What's wrong?"

"Your mother has been calling up here all morning." *Damn.* I leaned in closer trying to hear. "She says you don't have her permission to have this procedure."

"But, I'm seventeen. I don't need her permission."

"Typically, you wouldn't. But she's threatening to send the police to get you and treat you as a truant. We're supposed to call her if you show up here."

"This is unbelievable."

"I'm sorry, but we're not going to be able to perform this procedure for you today." She looked at me as if she expected me to say "Okay" and walk away. But that wasn't about to happen.

"Look, the law says I don't have to have her permission. I've waited the required amount of time, and I don't have a lot more time to do this before it's going to be too late. You have to help me." My voice trembled, but I refused to cry. Other patients had put down their magazines and were watching the exchange.

"Just a moment," the receptionist said, picking up the telephone beside her computer.

Five minutes later, the familiar blonde with the clip board appeared at the desk. She took me to an office approximately the size of a walk-in closet, and offered me a seat in a cheap gray swivel chair pushed against a wall. A pleasant lady in a blue sweater and pearls sat behind the faux walnut desk that occupied most of the room.

"Ms. Sumner," she said without preamble, "that was your mother on the phone. She is adamant that you not be allowed to have an abortion. Why do you think that is?"

"I don't know," I said with a scowl, my arms folded across my chest in frustration. "I guess she wants me to have this baby, quit school, get on welfare and food stamps, and live with her for the rest of my life. She's had two abortions herself; did she tell you that?" The sudden memory of having accompanied Mama to this same building as a little girl and taking care of her in the aftermath put a lump in my throat. "I don't know why she's doing this to me." By the time I finished the sentence, I was crying again.

The lady offered me a tissue from the box on her desk. I took two and blew my nose, trying to compose myself. She read my chart.

"Tell me about your home life," she said gently. We talked for several minutes about Mama and Margaret Ann and Johnny Ray. We talked about my runaway experience three years earlier. I told her about Vanderbilt and my dream of being a writer. She asked about Andy and church and God. It actually felt good to talk it all out with someone.

"Well, Ms. Sumner, you seem to have a good head on your shoulders. You've given your life and this decision a lot of thought. It's not going to be easy, no matter what you choose to do. But if you're certain that you want to end this pregnancy, we'll move forward."

"Oh, thank you so much." I beamed, resisting the urge to hug the woman.

She smiled, and then asked, "How did you get to the clinic?"

"I rode the bus."

"I was afraid of that. We can perform the procedure, but we can't allow you to go home alone on the bus. You'll need someone here to actually sign you out." She paused searching my face. "Is there someone you can call?"

I hesitated. I'd come this far. "Yes." I used the telephone on her desk to call Aunt Grace. "I'm on my way," she said before I could finish explaining.

"Good," the lady said, having heard the conversation. "Leslie will take you back out to the lobby now. We'll call you in shortly."

140

Everyone looked up when I opened the door to the lobby. I smiled shyly and took a new seat as the one I'd been in earlier was occupied by a new girl.

CHAPTER THIRTY-ONE

After just a couple of minutes, the nurse called my name and escorted me to exam room four. The stark room was large and cold, and, as I soon found out, so was the doctor. Dr. Fitz came in after I had dressed in the paper gown, opened down the front.

His first movement was to unceremoniously yank out the stirrups and flippantly motion for me to put my feet inside. His drawn face looked as if he'd been sucking lemons. His behavior turned my nervousness into fear and threw my stomach into turmoil.

"Is it going to hurt?" I finally worked up the nerve to ask.

"Just some pressure," he said off-handedly as he inserted the speculum without warning.

"Aw!" I said, scowling at him. He made a guttural sound as if disgusted with me. I looked for the nurse. I could see her out of the corner of my eye. She was putting items out on a table. "Could you hold my hand?" I asked her.

"No," replied the doctor, before she could answer. "She's here to assist me, not coddle you."

I sucked in a breath as he inserted something I couldn't see.

"This hurts," I said, tears starting to trickle down my left cheek.

"I'm just opening your cervix. If you can't take this little bit of pressure, then maybe we should stop the procedure now."

The harshness of his words bruised my heart. They held no kindness. I laid still and tried to remove myself from the room. I tried to focus on something pleasant, but I couldn't think of anything. Then I heard a sound that made me nearly jump out of my skin. It sounded vaguely like a vacuum cleaner. The hum of it seemed to vibrate the room.

"Hold still," the doctor commanded impatiently.

"What is that?" I asked frantically, hoping for some assurance that it had nothing to do with me.

"It's the suction devise," he said as if I was stupid.

The pain of it suppressed the other stupid questions I had. Determined not to scream, I let out a low, steady moan. I didn't know that I would be able to feel the machine literally suck the baby out of me.

"Oh, Jesus," I cried silently. "Jesus, please forgive me." I didn't make another sound. Alone in the responsibility for what I'd done, the pain was mine to bear. I would carry it with me for the rest of my life.

When the doctor finished, he simply left the room. No instruction. No encouragement. No discussion.

"Lay here for a few minutes," the nurse said gently. "When you feel like sitting up, we'll move you into the recovery room." She patted my hand, and then left me alone. I took a deep breath and pushed myself up. I felt battered and dizzy. I leaned toward the trashcan and threw up. The nurse must've heard me, because she came back. She steadied me, and then gave me some pills and a paper cup filled with water.

"Take these. They're for the pain." I wondered if she meant the pain in my heart. I nodded, then swallowed the pills, put down the cup and got dressed. She led me into a room of a half dozen lazy boy chairs. I eased into one and was asleep instantly. The next thing I knew she was waking me.

"Alright, Ms. Sumner, you can go home now."

I felt as if I'd been asleep for hours, but needed days more rest. I struggled to my feet and was once again overcome with dizziness. I found the trashcan just in time. I looked up at the nurse with raised eyebrows.

"Yes, it's normal."

I seemed to float out of the building. I hardly remember seeing Aunt Grace, or being handed the medicine, or anything about the drive home. I must have slept the entire way. I couldn't walk up the stairs to our apartment alone, so Aunt Grace let me lean on her. When Mama opened the door, Aunt Grace said something to her, then walked me to my room and put me in bed. I don't know what happened after that.

I woke the next morning groggy and thick. I struggled out of bed and into the bathroom. My stomach cramped so badly and there was so much blood, I thought I would surely die. Mama saw me in the hallway.

"You'd better hurry up and get dressed. Today is a school day, remember?" she said sarcastically.

"I remember."

"Then get ready. You love school so damn much you need to get on up there."

"Mama, I'm sick."

"Oh no, you're not sick, Kathy. Let's call it what it is."

"I'm sick."

"No, you had an abortion! You took your grown ass up there and did exactly what I told you not to do. You told me you were going to school. You lied to me, Kathy, and now you want my sympathy. Well, there's no sympathy for you!"

"And you never have had any, so, why should this be any different?"

"Don't you raise your voice at me! This is my house and as long as you're in it, you'll do as I say."

"Then maybe I should leave!" I threw up, and then rinsed my mouth while she watched from the doorway. I pushed past her, went into my room, slammed the door, and called Aunt Grace.

"Can you come get me, please?" I asked when she answered on the second ring.

"Kathy?"

"Yeah."

"What happened?"

"Nothing. I'm fine. Mama's just going crazy and I can't handle it right now."

"Alright, I'm on my way. I'll be there in twenty minutes." She hung up and I got dressed. After stuffing some clothes in a paper sack, I waited for her on the couch in the living room.

"And just where the hell do you think you're going?" Mama barked coming into the room, seeing the bag.

"Away from here."

"You ain't going no goddamned where. Do you hear me? No where." Aunt Grace's car horn sounded.

"Mama, I'm weak; I hurt; and I need to rest. I can't do that here. I'm going to stay with Aunt Grace for a few days. I'll be back."

"I told you, you're not going anywhere."

I had moved to the door. She stood a foot away from me with her hands on her hips and a fierce look on her face. I twisted the knob.

"If you walk out that door, you cannot come back. I mean it. I will never forgive you." Deathly calm, her eyes were cold and hard.

I opened the door and waved Aunt Grace off. "It's okay," I yelled from the doorway. "I'm staying here."

I watched her drive away and as her car grew smaller and smaller, so did my hope that I would ever be well again.

CHAPTER THIRTY-TWO

The next morning I awoke determined to go to school and get my life back to normal. Every step I took hurt somewhere, but I grimaced and continued to put one foot in front of the other. I could not spend another day with Mama glaring at me. So, if school was the only alternative, then to school I would go.

Jonetta was waiting for me at the end of the driveway and I was actually glad to see her. That was until she punched me – hard – in the arm.

"Hey!" I recoiled. "What was that for?"

"For deserting me these last few weeks."

I was guilty as charged. Jonetta was my best friend and while she had other people to hang out with, walking to school was something only we could do together given that ours were the last two apartment complexes in our school's eastern boundaries, and we were the only seniors living in either complex.

"I'm sorry," I said. "I've been really sick."

"I figured that's what was going on since you've missed so many classes. Glad you're feeling better."

She gave me the once over. "Are you feeling better?" she asked with raised eyebrows.

I must not have looked like it. "Yeah," I said trying to sound more energetic than I felt. "I'm definitely feeling better."

"Good!" Jonetta tucked her arm around mine, "You've missed so much!"

As we walked, she talked non-stop and I was alright with that. I needed to get out of my own head and leave the problems I'd been dealing with and return to the world around me. Jonetta filled me in on all the latest happenings. Her basketball team was playing in the regional. How had I missed that? Amy and Kyle were no long sitting together in the cafeteria, which didn't bode well for their relationship status. And Pete has been selected to serve on the prom planning committee. The four of us – Pete, Richard, Jonetta and I – planned to attend together and having one of us serve on the committee meant that the rest of us would have to help out. That might even be fun.

Going up the steps of the main building, Jonetta stopped. "Oh!" she said excitedly. "I forgot to tell you."

"What?"

"Today is Scholarship Announcement Day! You have to turn in your scholarship award letters to the main office and they're going to announce them in senior assembly this afternoon."

"Oh."

"What? You didn't bring yours? That's okay. The guidance counselors get copies of all the letters. They'll have yours on file. They just wanted us to submit ours in case we got one that they didn't get a copy of."

"No, it's not that." I paused. "I don't think I got any letters. Did you?"

"Well, yeah. You know I got that basketball scholarship to Jackson State. And remember the partial academic scholarship I got from Tougaloo College? I turned both of those letters in yesterday."

I smiled at her excitement. "Of course, it just slipped my mind. I am still recovering, you know."

"Yeah, I can tell."

College was the talk of the day. Pete had received a full scholarship to the University of Tennessee and Richard had been accepted into West Point Military Academy. Jonetta was likely to take the basketball scholarship to Jackson State, which meant that all my friends were going off somewhere after graduation. They would all start on their life's journey in other cities with new friends to make and new things to learn.

But, what about me? Why hadn't I gotten any letters? I hadn't even been offered a partial scholarship anywhere. It didn't make sense. I'd gotten early acceptance letters to two colleges before Christmas. Had they found out about what happened and changed their minds? Was I destined to live at home with my mother forever? These thoughts swirled around in my mind throughout the day and remained with me as I walked with my friends from our last class of the day to the gymnasium for senior assembly.

On the dais sat the usual suspects: our principal, Mr. Rogers, Dr. Hunter, and all three guidance counselors. With them were four men and two women who were not familiar. No students were on the stage. This was serious business.

Mr. Rogers addressed the class. "Ladies and gentlemen, it is my pleasure to announce that this senior class has earned $11.8 million in scholarships!"

We erupted into cheers. There was a lot of pint up energy to release and we clapped and hooted and hollered for several minutes. Reclaiming control, Mr. Rogers continued. "Many of our students earned more than one scholarship and some were awarded different types of scholarships. For example, we have scholar athletes who earned sports scholarship as well as academic scholarships."

"We have band members and cheerleaders and drama students who have earned recognition for both their extracurricular activities as well as their academic success. In other words, we have a talented student body with choices to make and I, as your principal, couldn't be more proud."

Again, my classmates celebrated. But this time I didn't join in. I had nothing to celebrate; I had no choices to make; and I had nothing to be proud about.

Mr. Rogers cleared his throat. "Before our guidance counselors come forward to read the names and amounts of each of our scholarship recipients, Dr. Hunter will introduce our special guests."

"Good afternoon," Dr. Hunter intoned.

"Good afternoon," we recited.

"Each scholarship offer you've received – however large or small, to whichever college or university, partial or full, sports, extracurricular, or academic – is special and worthy of celebrating. Each of these awards is a testament to your diligence, your perseverance, your talent, your skill, and, in some cases, your sheer determination. You have all worked very hard and these offers are your reward. They are your tickets to a bright and successful future."

"Most of you learned about your scholarship offers through letters mailed to your home. Copies of these letters were also sent to your guidance counselors here at the school. However, at many colleges and universities, there are certain scholarship offers that are also made in person."

"Behind me are representatives from six such institutions of higher learning: Tulane University in New Orleans, the University of Kentucky in Louisville, Washington University in St. Louis, the University of

Tennessee in Knoxville, Vanderbilt University in Nashville, and our city's very own University of Memphis. Each of these representatives is here to offer his or her respective institution's highest ranking and most coveted scholarships, which, by the way, are all inclusive. That means the education is free, the books are free, the dorms are free, and even some of the meals are free. Now that's a scholarship!"

Again, we applauded. That was certainly the type of scholarship I needed. I think I clapped the loudest. Dr. Hunter put his hands up to quiet the class. "Each representative will step to the podium and call out the student who has earned their most prestigious honor. If your name is called, please come quickly to the stage to accept your award."

Wasting no time, a tall, thin woman with long, blonde hair stood first. The black pencil skirt she wore was topped off with a fitted, v-neck fuchsia sweater. In a sweet southern drawl she announced, "Tulane University awards its Chairman's Scholarship to Miss Amy Winters."

The beauty queen surprise-look was immediate. Amy stood and waved to her adoring crowd. The popular clique out-cheered everyone and Amy was clearly in her element. She would fit in nicely at Tulane.

As Amy mounted the stairs, a short, balding man announced the Board of Regents Scholarship winner for the University of Kentucky. It went to Kyle. Wow. I raised an eyebrow at Jonetta. I guessed that was the end of that great romance. Maybe they already knew they were going in different directions. That could explain why they were no longer taking lunch together.

The Washington University representative took the podium to announce that their Psychology Chair of Excellence Scholarship recipient would be Heather Smith. Hmm, I thought. The three of them were also being split

apart by college, just like Jonetta, Richard, Pete and me.
Now I didn't feel quite so alone. Still, they were all going
to college and I was going no where. I had no offers. But
the woman from Vanderbilt was here. Maybe, I thought,
just maybe there was a chance. I crossed my fingers.

When things quieted down, the man from the
University of Tennessee stood to announce that their
Leadership Scholarship was being given to Peter Lewinsky.
"Pete!" I shouted. "You got one!" He beamed, then put his
hand to the side of his mouth and whispered, "That's what
my scholarship letter said," before leaving the bleachers to
take his place on the stage. So they did know.

I took a deep breath and sat up taller as the
Vanderbilt representative stepped to the microphone.
Maybe my letter had been lost in the mail. Those things
happened. The brown wavy-haired woman wore a dark
tailored pinstripe suit and spoke with authority. I would
definitely fit in there, I thought. "Vanderbilt University is
pleased to present its Scholar of Distinction award to Justin
Davis." My heart sank. Justin was a good guy and all but
his family had money. They could send him to Vanderbilt
without a scholarship. Mama couldn't send me to the store
some days. Ugh. I wanted to crawl under the bleachers. I
was doomed. What was I going to do?

My mind was numb and I was feeling drained. A
dull ache was rising from the pit of my stomach and into
my head. I paid little attention as the man representing the
University of Memphis began talking. "The Presidential
Scholarship is the highest award offered by the University
of Memphis," he droned, "and as Dr. Hunter said, it covers
all expenses. It is given to only one student each year – one
outstanding student. This year's scholarship recipient is
deserving in every way. Please join me in welcoming to
the stage and congratulating Miss Kathleen Sumner."
I gasped and jumped up. Jonetta didn't have to nudge me
that time. I'd heard my name. "Thank you, Jesus!" I

whispered. The tears were already rolling down my cheeks before I made it to the stage. I wasn't going to be left behind. I was going to have a choice. There was hope for me after all.

About the Author

Dorchelle Terrell Spence is a writer and communications professional who serves as Vice President for the Riverfront Development Corporation in Memphis, Tennessee. Spence also served as an adjunct professor at the University of Memphis, is a contributing writer to local and regional publications, and enjoys public speaking.

In 2013, Spence was named a Woman of Excellence by The New Tri-State Defender Newspaper. In 2003, she was recognized as one of the Top 40 Under 40 by The Memphis Business Journal and in 2001, she was named one of 50 Women Who Make a Difference by Memphis Woman magazine. Spence earned her MBA from the University of Memphis' prestigious Fogelman College of Business and Economics and is an alumnus of both Leadership Memphis and the New Memphis Institute.

A native Memphian, Spence is married, has one 12-year-old daughter, and three young adult stepsons. She is currently working on the sequel to No Less Worthy, taking her main character's journey beyond high school and into adulthood.

CPSIA information can be obtained at www.ICGtesting.com
Printed in the USA
LVOW10s0953240216

476258LV00004B/5/P

9 780981 532646